Chosen Pride

"I have definitely enjoyed this series and would recommend all three books."

—Joyfully Jay

"Fans of this unique take on shifters will undoubtedly enjoy this story as much as I did. I hope that we get to see more of this world because it's endlessly fascinating to me."

—The Novel Approach

When the Dust Settles

"Behind the light and fun surface, there're quite a few issues addressed here and all these details add up to a wonderful read you don't want to miss. Highly recommended!"

—Three Books Over The Rainbow

"Smokin' hot and such a wonderful treat for Mary Calmes's fans!"

—Hearts on Fire Reviews

Tied Up in Knots

"This story grabs you by the throat and doesn't let go. *Tied Up In Knots* is an absolute gem in this series, polished to a brilliant, glittering shine…"

—Gay Book Reviews

"I just love the combination of Calmes' writing style with her version of action and suspense. It's unbeatable in my opinion."

—Under the Covers Book Blog

By MARY CALMES

Published by DREAMSPINNER PRESS
www.dreamspinnerpress.com

A DAY MAKES

Mary Calmes

DREAMSPINNER
PRESS

Published by
DREAMSPINNER PRESS

5032 Capital Circle SW, Suite 2, PMB# 279, Tallahassee, FL 32305-7886 USA
www.dreamspinnerpress.com

A Day Makes
© 2017 Mary Calmes.

Cover Art
© 2017 Reese Dante.
http://www.reesedante.com
Cover content is for illustrative purposes only and any person depicted on the cover is a model.

ISBN: 978-1-63533-793-8
Digital ISBN: 978-1-63533-574-3
Library of Congress Control Number: 2017902302
Published April 2017
v. 1.0

Printed in the United States of America
∞
This paper meets the requirements of
ANSI/NISO Z39.48-1992 (Permanence of Paper).

Always for Lynn, and a huge thank-you to Susan,
who has given me a new place for many new characters to live.

What a diff'rence a day made
Twenty-four little hours
                    —María Grever

CHAPTER ONE

CERTAIN TIMES in my life I could remember like yesterday. Meeting Grigor Jankovic was one of them.

I had been so close to getting away.

I purchased a plane ticket to Jacksonville with the very last of my cash, and as I sat on the airport shuttle while it made its way to Departures at McCarran International—everything I owned shoved into a small duffel—I tried to be hopeful. One of the guys I'd served with had offered to put me up for a month in exchange for helping him out with some maybe-not-so-legal activities. And while Florida had not been on my list of places to go, I was completely out of options.

After getting off the tram, I was waiting to cross the street to the terminal when a car cut me off, making it impossible to step off the curb. Backpedaling, I took a quick breath, prepared to disappear forever. They would kill me right there and I would be just another statistic, a dead ex-Marine who'd fallen on hard times, made questionable decisions, and ended up shot in the street.

But when the window lowered, a face emerged instead of a gun.

All my life, my curiosity had gotten the better of me. So instead of bolting, I waited to see what would happen next.

"Grigor Jankovic wants to speak to you."

The first time I heard the man's name was after I took a gun from a guy who was aiming it at me and I killed him. Now, I was hearing it from a man in a car, in what sounded to me like a Russian or eastern European accent. I couldn't tell; I didn't know for certain. All I did know was that it was the same name that was supposed to inspire fear… and was doing a damn good job. I'd gotten from the guy I killed a week ago that Grigor would gut me, and his friend had snarled the same thing right before I blew his brains out too. They'd promised me death with their dying breaths, so to be faced with the apparent devil's minion was terrifying.

"He wants to put a bullet in me, you mean," I stated to the guy in the car.

"No," he corrected me. "Only meet."

I studied his face.

"You should take me at my word."

Maybe I looked stupid. People often felt they had to explain things to me more than once. Perhaps it was because I never just answered, instead always mulled my reply over before speaking, but I'd noticed most everyone felt compelled to fill the silence with the sound of their own voice.

"Well?"

"There's no way in hell I'm getting in that car so you can drive me to some out-of-the-way private location to be tortured and killed."

"Why would we do this?"

I shrugged, wishing I hadn't ditched the gun I'd taken off that guy in the convenience store after the knock-down drag-out fight with Jankovic's "associates." But I couldn't take it into the airport, and because I didn't want some kid to find it, I'd taken it apart, put one piece in the sewer and the other in a dumpster close by the crappy roach-infested motel I'd been staying at.

"You watch too many movies."

He'd caught me off-guard. "What?"

"I said," he sighed, "you watch too many movies. We *abduct* people we will torture and kill. We do not ask nicely for them to take ride."

"Is that right?"

"*Da.*"

I nodded even as I turned to bolt.

"Please do not make me chase you," came a second voice, this one deeper and rumbling. I realized I could actually tell the difference, now clearly hearing a Russian accent as opposed to whatever the first guy's was. "It will annoy me and start us off on wrong foot."

Pivoting, I saw the driver's side window had lowered, and the man there was scowling at me. He looked more dangerous than the one in the backseat. That guy had smiled, at least. This one had not.

"This is correct, yes? Wrong foot?"

"It is."

He nodded. "Good."

"So you were saying about your boss?"

"*Da*. Grigor," he went on. "He wants only to speak to you about your run-in with our colleagues, that is all."

I cleared my throat. "I have a plane to catch. It leaves in an hour."

He exhaled deeply, clearly bored. "We will get you new ticket, first-class ticket, you need only to come and speak to Grigor."

At which point the guy in the backseat—he looked good in his suit; the Italian wool blend surely cost more than everything I owned put together—got out and held open the door. The time to run had passed, so I swallowed down my fear and climbed in.

The ride was not what I expected. The guys kept up a running dialogue once I was inside, and what was nice was that even though English was most obviously their second (or more) language, they spoke it for me during the drive. What was even better was the way they ignored me, just talking instead about some guy who had pissed himself when Marko Borodin—the mean-looking one driving—had simply stopped to ask for directions.

"I keep telling you," the guy sitting beside me, who'd introduced himself as Pravi Radic, replied, "You are scary as fuck."

I would have agreed, but I didn't think they'd appreciate me chiming in.

"Do you not agree?" Pravi asked me.

Glancing around the car, I smiled slightly. "He could smile a bit more."

And everyone in the car lost it, which let me breathe. Just a little.

I was surprised when we reached a dive bar off the strip because, I'd been sure, even with the reassurances, that I was being taken to an empty warehouse or somewhere else along those lines. But instead, only Pravi and I got out and walked into a pub with sticky floors, one TV over the bar, and a lot of wood paneling.

Toward the back, in one of the cheap vinyl booths, was a man sitting alone.

"That is Grigor," Pravi informed me, in case I couldn't tell.

Here was the guy I'd been trying to avoid since I put two of his men in the ground and three more in the hospital a week ago.

When I reached the table, I stood there for a moment, looking down at Jankovic before he noticed me hovering and gestured for me to take a seat. Once we were eye to eye, he offered me a cigarette that I refused and then asked if I wanted something to drink.

I cleared my throat. "I would prefer if you just went ahead and shot me, Mr. Jankovic, because waiting for it is probably gonna be worse than the bullet, at this point."

His thick black brows furrowed before he leaned sideways to look up at Pravi. "You didn't explain to him that I wanted to offer him a position within our organization?"

I was surprised. From the sound of his men, I'd been expecting Jankovic to have an accent as well. But he sounded like he'd gone to boarding school or college. He was definitely better educated than me.

Pravi only shrugged. "I thought perhaps you would want to say."

Jankovic groaned, letting his head tip slightly sideways while he took a long drag on his cigarette before grinding it out in the ashtray.

I was really confused.

"So, Ceaton—may I call you Ceaton, or do you prefer Mr. Mercer?"

"Ceaton is good."

"And I am Grigor," he said as he cleared his throat. "Now, Ceaton, shall I tell you what I did this morning?"

"Sure."

"I had to take care of the men you didn't kill."

This whole thing just kept getting weirder.

"You see," he sighed, lacing his fingers together, leaning forward to look me in the eye, "these are not the days of Al Capone and other infamous gangsters. Now business should be conducted quietly, discreetly, so no one is the wiser. If the FBI or the DEA or the ATF never learn my name, then I'm very pleased."

That made sense.

"But those men that you had the misfortune of dealing with were collecting protection money on the side."

When I'd heard threats as I stood in line at the small convenience store, waiting to buy the microwave burrito and Gatorade I could afford, I knew exactly what the men had been doing there. The clerk had been terrified and—

"Wait, on the side?" I asked when what he'd said hit me.

He grunted.

Something new was starting to take shape. "You don't collect protection money?"

"Not at that level," he replied, clearly disgusted.

"Oh," I said, smiling at him. "So those guys were using your name, collecting money, and not telling you."

"Correct."

"And you only found out about it when a couple of 'em turned up in the morgue."

"Yes," he agreed. "And when I learned that the rest of them were in the hospital, I dispatched two members of my crew to investigate."

There were levels in the mob, I knew that from watching *The Godfather* and *The Sopranos* and every other gangster movie. And yes, on the whole, they were movies about the Italian mob, but I figured the structure had to be similar. Basically there were your men, who made up the whole organization, and then there was your crew. The difference was that "men" meant whoever was on your payroll. Your "crew" were the guys you trusted with your life who would trade theirs for yours. Crew was brotherhood, was deeper, and it reminded me of what I'd shared with the guys I'd served with.

"Ceaton?"

"Sorry. What'd you find out?"

"Precisely what I suspected from the moment I found out where they died."

"Okay, but what does this have to do with me?"

"Two men buried, three in the hospital," he reiterated.

"Yeah."

His smile made his eyes gleam. "You are a man of many talents, Ceaton, and I would be foolish to pass up this opportunity to offer you a place with me."

And then I saw it, in his face, an untightening and an ease. His shoulders relaxed, too, and he took a breath.

"You don't even know me," I reminded him.

"But I have an idea," he explained. "Because you saved those people who owned that store from my men, but you didn't turn in my men that you didn't kill."

"What?"

"You did what was necessary. Even in the heat of the moment, you kept your wits about you. I can use a man like that."

"I'm not exactly a good Samaritan, Mr. Janko—"

"Grigor," he corrected me.

"Grigor," I parroted. "I've done—"

"Oh yes, I know," he conceded. "Because think about the terrible position you put those people in—the ones who owned the store."

"I'm sorry?"

He shrugged. "You were leaving the state with no concern for them beyond the events of the day."

"I don't—"

"What if those men came back to settle the score, and you weren't there to help a second time?"

That had never occurred to me.

"Did you once stop to think of what the fallout would be and how they would deal with it without you there?"

I watched as one of his eyebrows lifted.

"You didn't think."

I hadn't, he was right. I'd been too set on my course to the exclusion of all else. I always worked in the moment, never concerning myself with long-term anything.

"Perhaps it's because you have no home, no roots," he suggested. "If you did, you might think more long-term."

He had a point.

"So maybe working for me wouldn't just be you doing me a favor."

I remained quiet.

"Tell me something. Where did you learn to fight like you do?"

"Marine Corps."

"And why aren't you still serving?"

"It's a long story."

"Excellent," he assured me. "Those are my favorites."

"Don't you have things to do?"

He shook his head. "Nothing more important than this."

I had to think of what to say.

"Just tell the story," he suggested when he noticed me deliberating.

I'd been a scout sniper in the Marine Corps. As such, I was normally either above the action, covering the men on the ground like an angel of death ready to kill anyone who got too close to my team, or out with my observer doing reconnaissance at a safe distance. The day my career ended, my unit was covering another, providing protection for an Army Black Ops team that had been sent to assassinate an enemy target.

From our position on the roof of a building in a rundown industrial zone close to the slums of southern Fallujah, in the early predawn hours, Corporal Michael Tanner, my observer—my lookout, my targeter, my new partner I didn't know very well yet though he seemed like a solid guy—saw a white pickup gaining speed as it drove through the decimated streets littered with sewage and trash. When another pulled in behind it, I called down to my lieutenant and told him they had to hunker down because they were about to have company. I was stunned when moments later he ordered the team to move out.

My breath caught. "Say again, sir?"

"Cover us, Mercer; we're heading for the back door."

But the team we were there to see to safety was still at least another ten minutes from our position, and they were on foot. We had the helicopters on standby, ready to meet our two-vehicle convoy of a wrecker and a Humvee; they did not. They just had us. If we bailed, they'd be sitting ducks without transport.

"Sir, be advised that Gold Team is—"

"That's an order, Mercer, now move your ass!"

I cleared my throat. "Request permission to remain behind, sir, and wait for—"

"I need you to guard our six."

"I can do both, sir," I assured him. "From where I am I—"

"I better not have to tell you again!" he roared at me. "I expect you here now!"

I exchanged glances with Tanner—and in that moment, I understood I had a choice. Right then, right there, I could follow orders or I could do what was right. My people were entrenched and hidden, but Gold Team would be out in the open, exposed and vulnerable. But even with that, even though I outranked Tanner, I had to let him make his choice before I responded.

"Mercer!"

I gestured for Tanner to go and then nodded to reinforce the idea that it was okay for him to leave me.

He shook his head and then looked away from me like it was settled.

"No, sir," I replied then.

"Say again, Marine?"

"No. Sir."

"Mercer—"

"It'll be like shooting fish in a barrel, sir. I cannot leave them unprotected."

"Oh, but leaving us out here with our dicks hanging in the wind, that's okay."

"No, sir, but from where you are—"

"They'll court martial you for this, Mercer."

There absolutely was that possibility. I would have agreed, but at that moment the roof I was on was hit with strafing gunfire from the next building over.

I broke cover and ran flat out for the stairs, Tanner on my heels. If I hadn't had the gun, we could have leaped from the building we were on to the next, but not with my M40A1. If I fell and rolled, if the rifle took any damage—I just couldn't chance it. So I went for the door instead.

"Mercer! Mercer!"

With my lieutenant yelling in my ear, Tanner trying to contact the gunny, shots going off around me, and then explosions—there was no missing the damage from an RPG—the only thing I knew was that we had to get to the cover position for the rendezvous with Gold Team and save them from what was shaping up to be an ambush.

By the time we reached the bottom of the stairs and darted sideways so we wouldn't run directly out into the street, there was only fire and ash. Even with loud, angry orders being screamed at me to turn around, I made my way to the spot where we were supposed to meet the team. I had a moment of terror when I realized it was just me and Tanner, but that vanished when I saw the members of Gold Team moving slowly, carefully through the now smoky streets, sticking to the darkness, the sunrise being just far enough away to grant them the cover they desperately needed.

I hugged the walls, clutching my rifle in one hand, my M9 Beretta in the other, making my way through the cesspit of streets that I felt sorry people had to live in every day. The country was ravaged by war, and my fondest wish was that the conflict could just simply stop and the government would say, shit, yeah, we should take care of our people. But the reality of any disagreement was that it absolutely made sense—depending on the side you were on. I couldn't even imagine an end. But at the moment, the people I'd come to save were my main objective.

When we were a half a block away, my cell phone buzzed in the breast pocket of my vest, which startled the hell out of me.

"Mercer," came the greeting, the silky rumble of the man's voice spreading calm over my raw nerves. "This is Gold Leader."

I wasn't even going to ask. They were Special Ops, Black Ops, scary kill-you-in-your-sleep ops. The point was not how the man got my number, but why he hadn't called earlier. "Sir."

"Where's the rest of our protection?"

I looked at Tanner before sort of telling the truth. "They had to take cover, sir."

He grunted.

"Don't go near the rendezvous point, sir, it's all compromised. Everything is."

"Do you know the way out?"

"Yessir. Follow me."

So they all crossed, quieter than I thought men carrying that much hardware could, and we made our way in and out, around, down alleys, along the sides of burned out buildings, until the main road was visible. I heard the whistle right before the blast, and then I was on one side, Gold Team on the other, screaming at them to get down, swearing I had not led them into a firefight. I knew where safety was—we just weren't there yet.

The sky lit up seconds later.

"Follow me, Mercer," Gold Leader ordered, and I would have, truly would have, if the street hadn't seemingly lifted up and then dropped back down, reordered, in different alignment, in fire and smoke and falling debris.

Tanner and I were thrown back into a wall and that was all. I never saw the team or my observer again.

"Holy shit," Grigor breathed.

I'd forgotten he was listening, lost in the telling of it. "I—sorry. That was more than you wanted to know, I'm sure."

He leaned closer. "That was amazing."

I opened my mouth to say something.

"So I don't understand. Why didn't you get a medal?"

"Tanner died," I said sadly, remembering his face as I always did, his pale blue eyes and straw-colored hair.

"Yes, but—"

"See, the second I said no—I was fucked. Tanner died," I repeated hollowly, "and I was in the hospital so there was no one to speak up for me when the lieutenant filed charges."

"But you saved those men."

"It didn't matter. I went against my lieutenant's orders and my partner was killed."

His eyes were searching my face, waiting to hear more.

"So, because I did it to save the other team, they didn't automatically court martial me. The Marines don't do things that way. We don't leave our men behind. Semper Fi. But my choice got a man on my team, my partner, killed. So they gave me the choice between court martial and quiet discharge. I took the discharge. And even though they don't call it a dishonorable discharge anymore, that's what it means. So any plans I had to go into law enforcement when I got out were basically screwed."

"All because you did what was *right*."

"It's what *I* thought was right, yeah. I mean, my lieutenant, he probably thought it was completely wrong, and from his side…." I thought about it as I had a million times. "No, he was safe, the other guys were safe, the only ones who were stuck out there with their dicks in the wind was Gold Team."

"So in your heart, you know you made the right decision."

"Yeah." I agreed.

Really, in the end, I figured they were right to boot me out. Tanner died because I kept him from leaving when we had orders to retreat. I'd given him the option to go, to follow the lieutenant's orders, but he was my observer, he knew his place was by my side, and he'd trusted me to make the right choice.

"So you can sleep well knowing that."

"It doesn't bring Tanner back."

"No. But didn't he agree with you?"

"How do you mean?"

"Asked outright, he would have said yes, saving those men is the right thing to do. He knew what was on the line."

"He knew. He was a Marine just like me."

"Then when he followed you, when he remained at your side, he knew that choice could cost him his life."

"That doesn't absolve me."

"No, *and* yes. Having never been in combat, I suspect that the decisions are split-second ones and the consequences need to be sorted out afterwards."

"True."

His eyes narrowed as he studied me. "So you regret losing your partner that day, of course, but is there anything else?"

I nodded.

"Tell me."

"I wish—I never got a chance to contact the soldier in charge—Gold Leader—to see if they were okay. I tried to find out, but I was basically in the brig the second I got out of the hospital and no one ever told me shit."

"You were wounded?"

"Yeah, I got blown up, remember?"

"You look fine to me."

"There was a lot of stuff broken, believe me, but all in all, I was a helluva lot luckier than a lot of guys."

"Yes," he agreed.

"It's weird to have a plan and then see it changed in a matter of minutes."

He nodded. "Well, I think your life is about to change again right in front of your eyes."

"Is it?"

"Yes. Yes, it is."

I took a breath.

"Come on, let's get out of here. I'm starving. I feel like having breakfast."

My stomach growled at the mere mention. "Somewhere good?"

"The best," he promised.

It was amazing. He took me to his Aunt Jaja's house. The mansion was a neo-Mediterranean monolith with an infinity pool the size of a small lake, stables, tennis courts, and an outdoor cooking pit that was her favorite amenity. She showed me where a suckling pig was roasting slowly on a spit and then took me into her kitchen, sat me down, made me an espresso, and watched me eat homemade pastries that had everything from jam to salted meat inside.

"Who takes care of you?" she wanted to know, and unlike her nephew, there was a trace of the same accent all the others had besides Marko.

I shook my head.

"No? No family?"

Again, same motion.

"Your mother?"

"There's nobody."

"No wife?"

I cleared my throat because, really, at least I'd die with a full stomach if this was a problem. After glancing over at Grigor, I answered her. "It would be a man."

"Ah," she said, which surprised the hell out of me. "Like Oli."

"Oli?" I delved.

"My nephew," she sighed. "So pretty that one, so smart. He and his husband have two of the most beautiful girls you have ever seen. One adopted two years ago and one last year." Her smile spread from ear to ear, and then it slowly became a smirk. "I was out with them at a restaurant not long ago, and this whore, she says to my nephew, you are filth to raise those girls and keep them from having a mother."

"I'm sorry. Some people are ignorant."

She nodded. "This is true. But usually, if you do not know something, you stay quiet until you know enough to speak."

I chuckled. "If only."

She reached out and patted my face before settling back and folding her arms. "But you see, Oli and Ben—that is his husband—they are so good, so full of love for their angels. You should see how patient they are, how kind. In my day you spanked, but Oli, he says there is no place for hitting." She huffed out a breath. "I disagree."

I could tell she didn't mean the girls. "What'd you do?"

Quick shrug from her. "That woman who spoke shit? I followed her to the bathroom and broke her nose."

This was a surprise. "Really?"

She winked at me. "No one insults my family."

"I promise to keep that in mind."

"No. Already I can tell, you are a good boy. I have no worries for you."

I glanced at Grigor. "So it sounds like me being gay…."

Aunt Jaja waved a dismissive hand. "Why would he care? He is not to fuck girls in front of you; you will not fuck boys in front of him. All is good. You must simply protect the family like the rest of us. This is all he can ask of you."

Grigor shrugged and nodded and told me to come sit with him in the living room so we could talk. Later, as we were all watching football and eating snacks I had asked to help with, Jaja came in, kissed the top of my head, and then went back to the kitchen where several other women were now convened.

I watched her go, bemused, and turned to Grigor. "Can I ask a question?"

"Of course," he answered, not sparing me a look, too interested in the game.

"What kinda name is Jankovic?"

"Serbian."

"And that's what everybody's speaking."

"There is some Croatian as well, and every now and then Jaja throws in some Hungarian."

"Okay." I chuckled because he was still answering without actually giving me any real attention. He was taking me for granted already. I decided I liked it, a lot.

"Here," Grigor said and proceeded to hand me a Beretta PX4 Storm G21 semiautomatic with a holster. It was a beautiful gun, and so I looked to him.

"It's my gun, registered to me," he explained, finally turning his head. "So be careful where you leave it and who you shoot with it."

I was overwhelmed. It was a lot of trust, and I didn't know why he would give that to me so soon after our first meeting.

"You don't even know me," I said, trying to pass the weapon back to him.

He lifted his hand. "I know enough already. I've listened to you talk to the others, I've seen you trying to help Jaja. You need a family, Ceaton. We're going to be yours."

And since he was more right than he knew, I had Marko help me put on the holster and settled in, sat there on the couch and ate and bantered and finally breathed when Pravi, who was standing behind me, put a hand on my shoulder and left it there until the next play.

I hadn't felt protected and part of a family since I left the Marines. It was good to not be scared anymore.

CHAPTER TWO

BEING MOB muscle was probably not a lot of people's idea of being safe and sound, but for me, it was grounding. There's comfort in knowing exactly what you're supposed to be doing at any given moment. It's what I loved about being in the Marines, the lack of questions. Being on Grigor's payroll was similar. I knew what to do when I got up, where to go, who to check in with, and that I was to follow up with Grigor if I found any issues.

What started out as me standing in the background, listening, watching, changed over the past eighteen months to me leading. Grigor grew to trust me to get things done without him having to be there with me or me having to check in with him. I was not a guy who needed to be micromanaged, and he appreciated that. Since he traveled almost exclusively with Doran Loncar, who was in charge of his protection, that left me, Pravi, Marko, and Luka Novak to do the things Grigor preferred not to dirty his hands with.

For instance, Grigor didn't want to talk to the drug pushers. He had no interest in meeting them, handing out the product, or making sure that what was sold and the money that came in balanced. Marko wasn't terribly patient with that either. I'd been surprised that there was a Russian in Grigor's inner circle, once I figured out that everyone else was Serbian, and it turned out that Marko was just as amazed by my inclusion.

"How did you start working for Grigor?" I asked Marko one day, drunk enough that I was brave and sober enough to process the answer.

"Grigor and my old boss, they wanted to do business, but there was no trust."

"Sure."

"So they switched us, me for him. I would protect Grigor; Grigor's man Todor, he would protect Bohdan."

"But?"

He leaned forward on the table, looking at me, and I realized he was sloshed too. "Todor, he was no good, and Bohdan died choking on own blood."

"What'd you do?"

"I gut Todor and killed man who came after Grigor in the night."

"Did whoever took over for Bohdan want you back?"

He lifted his brows to indicate the yes. "But already, my loyalty was for Grigor. If I went back—with new boss there, I start at bottom."

"That sucks."

"*Da.*"

I blinked. "How come 'yes' is the same in Serbian and Russian?"

He stared at me.

"That's weird, right?"

He tipped his head back and forth like, maybe.

"We're bonding, am I right?"

The look I got told me the jury was still out, but that was okay. We were the two odd ducks, the two everyone else gave the side-eye to when they first met us, which, of course, made us closer. He was the one I ended up taking with me whenever I went to talk to club owners, another thing Grigor didn't like to do.

Collecting protection money on a large scale was something Grigor approved of. Nothing small, no mom-and-pop gas stations, no diners, no quaint little bed and breakfasts. Big dance clubs, lounges, restaurants, and anyone who owned a string of something like car dealerships, food trucks, check-cashing places were fair game. He liked funds rolling in, but again, going to those places, showing his face, was not his bag.

Not that I blamed him. As the head of the Serbian mob in Las Vegas, making deals with drug cartel kingpins was more glamorous than collecting money from pimps, running down leads from guys who stole guns or product from us, or killing people. With me in charge of those efforts, Grigor drew further and further away from anything remotely criminal. And while no one was stupid enough to think that Grigor Jankovic was completely on the up-and-up, he couldn't be directly tied to anything particularly illegal... at least on paper. The dirt had to be excavated, and since no one could get a warrant to do any digging, he looked really good from the outside.

He made huge real estate deals to buy and sell hotels as well as investments in startups, casinos he had his fingers in, and the stock market. He built a wing in the local children's hospital that he got to do the ribbon cutting for when it opened. He donated a shit-ton of money to the symphony and got his own private box, and he really enjoyed flipping mansions. Not big houses, but actual mansions that sold in the millions. When he took over a strip mall that turned into an urban renewal project, he couldn't be seen in public with me and the others anymore. Only his lawyer, his accountant, and Doran were allowed in photographs with him. The rest of us were a little too shady.

When he was invited to a fundraiser for the mayor, I thought Marko was going to choke on his laughter.

"What?" Pravi asked.

"Is so—" Marko looked at me, gesturing with his fingers, searching for the word in English. "How do you say—against what is right?"

"Hypocritical?"

"*Da.*"

Pravi nodded. "He doesn't do his own killing."

"That's what we're for," I told him.

On his way out the following night, before he left in the limousine in his Armani tuxedo with his socialite tobacco heiress girlfriend on his arm, he stopped and passed me a box. I got a pat on the cheek, and then he was gone.

Inside, there was a nickel-plated Armscor Rock Island Armory M1911A1 with pearl grips. It was gorgeous, and just like the one he carried. I was very touched.

"Is pussy gun," Marko said at dinner later that night after we'd made our runs. Luka Novak, who had joined the crew right before me, still lived at home with his mother, and when we dropped him off—or tried to—she always made sure we had a little something to eat before we went home.

At the moment, she was bustling around the table, having made goulash that smelled like heaven, cheese rolls, and Salcici—sort of a puffed pastry filled with jam—for dessert.

"She's cooking too much for us," I told Luka, smiling up at Mrs. Novak as she stopped behind me, put her hands on my face, and then pressed a kiss to my cheek.

"What about my nice nephew, Ceaton. He asked after you last Friday after Mass."

I whimpered and looked at Luka, who pretended to be very interested in his roll.

"Oh, Ma, the cheese in here is so good."

She was delighted and flitted off to get him a couple more.

"You should have never told anyone you were gay," Pravi stated. "It was a mistake. Now all the mothers who have a son who doesn't want to get married to a woman have their sights set on you."

"Was mistake," Marko agreed.

"At least they're trying to get me laid," I chimed in. "That's nice."

"They're trying to get you married," Pravi said, enlightening me. "Which is not so nice."

The issue was, besides the occasional blind date, I wasn't seeing anyone at all. There wasn't time. Much like the other guys, if I had an itch, if the lack of sex went so long that I thought I was going to die, then I'd find some guy willing and able to help me out. I got the occasional fuck, but what I did couldn't actually be classified as one-night stands because they never took that long.

I'd hooked up with men in bathrooms, in the backseat of cars, in alleys, and very rarely, in their apartments. It made no sense to follow someone all the way home and be leaving fifteen, twenty minutes later. It could have lasted longer, but I just wanted to get off and go. Kissing was a lost art with me; I had no interest, it took so much time. Fucking was about fast and dirty and hot and done.

I tried to want more from people, but no one held my interest at all. I never stopped dead in my tracks, overwhelmed by another person's beauty or allure. I noticed men, but no one made my whole body go still in anticipation of the next words out of their mouth. I'd never stood transfixed in another person's glow.

Not that I didn't want to find a man who made me look at him twice. I had dreams of finding *the one*, the guy who would care as much about my mind as he did about my body. I had the whole lazy Sunday morning fantasy going on, where making love and talking were spread out through the entire day.

But my reality was guys hanging upside down on meat hooks while Marko carved pieces out of them so their boss or their friends didn't fuck with Grigor. We had to intimidate and enforce, collect and distribute;

it was a full-time job that did not leave a lot of time for dating. What I realized, however, was that despite all that, I was still a romantic at heart. And while it was difficult, surrounded by death, by the solitary existence I led outside of work, I still took every corner wondering if this was the turn that would lead me to *the one*.

It wouldn't be easy, with the company I kept.

"You should not be married," Marko said, interrupting my thoughts. "To leave someone behind to bury you is not kind."

I shot him what I hoped was a pained look.

He scowled quickly. "Is true."

"Wouldn't it be worth it to find love?"

"For who?" He arched an eyebrow at me.

"And is it fair to drag a nice person into this life of guns and death?" Pravi posed. "I say no."

Both fair points.

Marko tipped his head at the new gun in my holster. "You should not carry that. People will try and take it from you for no good reason. A man who carries that kind of gun has small dick."

I smiled at him. "Grigor carries the same gun, asshole."

He shrugged and leaned sideways, lifting a gun from his ankle holster and passing it to me. It was a Sig Sauer P226. "Take this."

"I don't need a new gun, M," I assured him. "I have the one I got originally, and now I have one that's really fancy."

"Is too *fancy*," he declared, using my word, enunciating it and making it sound stupid. "And this one I give you, I have Osprey silencer that fits it. You need this."

I glanced over at Pravi, whose mouth was hanging open, and then at Luka, whose eyes were huge and round. I understood why. Marko didn't hand out firearms to just anyone.

Leaning sideways, I bumped against him and was surprised when he didn't let me straighten up instantly, instead curling his hand around my cheek and pressing me to his shoulder for a second. I had no idea he was capable of any sort of warmth at all, so really, I was as shocked as the others.

I told Grigor when I saw him the next afternoon how much I loved the gun but that carrying it would bring attention, even under my coat, and that wasn't a good idea. The idea was to be forgettable, not memorable in any way.

"So the gun is too pretty?"

"Yeah."

He squinted at me. "It's the same gun I carry."

"You seldom carry a gun anymore."

"True."

"And when you are strapped, I'm thinking you carry this one to be memorable. Am I right?" I asked, hoping it would make sense to him. I didn't want to hurt his feelings over the fact that I wasn't going to use his gift, but Marko was right. It was too flashy for me.

His nod, along with the smirk, made me laugh.

"You are not as easy to forget as you think," he assured me. "You're a handsome man, Ceaton Mercer. All the women ask after you."

I grunted.

"You're lucky you're gay, or I'd have to get rid of you."

"Oh?"

"No man wants to be in competition with his own, and I have enough problems already with Pravi."

He was right about that. Pravi gave new meaning to the words "smooth operator." The charm that oozed off that man was lethal. A few times there had been a woman on Grigor's arm who had watched Pravi with the eyes of a huntress. And even as I thought about the ridiculousness of the conversation, I saw how flat Grigor's stare had become as he gazed off into the distance.

He didn't like being second in any area of his life, and that included being the best-looking of us. I hadn't really considered the idea that his ego would extend to something so small and petty.

"Yeah, but you like your women classy," I commented, going with the pretext that we were just shooting the shit and that this wasn't, possibly, a life-and-death discussion for Pravi. "And your boy likes them easy."

It took a moment, but my words sank in, and he turned and grinned at me. "Yes, that's true. Pravi has a definite type."

I snorted out a laugh. "And it ain't the same as yours. Can you imagine Brooke Collingsworth looking twice at Pravi?"

She was Grigor's latest socialite, her father worth a cool billion.

"No," he replied smugly, "she would not."

I shrugged. "So who cares."

He nodded and gestured for me to sit with him.

I was about to do as he asked when the door opened and Jaja came rushing into the living room and over to Grigor. She grabbed his hand and told him that something was wrong with Sonya.

Normally Sonya, Jaja's youngest daughter, called Grigor every Sunday while he was hungover and watching soccer. They had been raised together, and he thought of her as more of a sister than a cousin. Because it was his veg day and the one day a week she didn't have classes or have to work, always, without fail, they spoke at some time between one and four. Now he looked at the time and saw that it was only three, so he told her not to worry.

"No," she insisted, her grip on his hand tightening. "A mother knows. I know."

He stared at his aunt for a moment and then turned to me. "Go check on Sonya."

"Going now," I agreed, getting on my phone and calling Pravi. "I'll call when we get there," I said to Grigor before I walked out the door.

Luka, Marko, Pravi, and I were on a plane for Boston two hours later.

ONCE WE hit town, Luka got us checked into a suite downtown on Court Street with a gorgeous view of the high rises. He stayed there to make calls, order in food, get the place stocked, and—most importantly—begin the database hacking he specialized in to find out what the police knew. He also searched hospitals and morgues, basically did whatever he could digitally. It wasn't my end. I was the door-to-door guy.

Other than the fact that she had met a friend to go clubbing Friday night—that was in her text log—we came up empty the night before when going through her phone after Luka hacked into it. Pravi and I were at the police station first thing Monday morning. We reported both Sonya and her friend Ellen missing, and they agreed to start looking for the girls.

"Are there any leads?" I asked the detective we finally sat down with after waiting half the day. It was why Marko hadn't come with us. The man had zero patience.

"We traced Ms. Crncevic's phone to a club called Carnal, so we're going there now to speak to the owner to try and see if he remembers her. Do you happen to have a recent picture?" Detective Geary asked me.

I had many.

While the police did their thing, the four of us hit the town. Luka checked into who owned the club, and once we found out it was a man named Kostya Beron, we started looking into who he was.

Marko and Pravi walked around the neighborhood the club was in and talked to people, handing out quite a bit of cash to keep their inquiries quiet while Luka and I tracked down where the money that came into the club flowed back out to. Luka did his online magic and found quite a few missing women associated with the location, and I kept an eye on everyone coming and going. In a short time, we had a better idea of what was going on inside after sitting on it the whole day. I recognized the signs.

"And?" Grigor asked when he picked up the phone.

"The place she was last seen at looks like Gen's club before we took it over."

He exhaled slowly. "So sex slaves and drugs?"

"Yeah."

"What does your gut say?"

I didn't want to say. "We have to wait and hear from the cops."

"That's not what I asked you."

"Let's not guess," I cautioned. "We need to know things concrete."

He cleared his throat. "Does it feel like Gen's club used to?"

"Yes," I said flatly.

After a moment he sniffed. "You were right about that change."

This was new. "Was I?"

"Yes, you were. I never wanted to be a pimp. Dancers are one thing, and what they choose to do with their own bodies—not my concern."

I had been with Grigor for three months when I went to him and said that I had to leave. I would not be in the business of prostitution. Finally trusted to see all facets of the business, I'd been horrified when I was taken to a string of high-end condos right off the strip to see the women there. Drugs, guns, murder for hire, protection, extortion, money laundering, blackmail, and loan sharking—all fine with me. But women, the sexual enslavement of anyone, boy or girl, was not something I could condone.

After leaving abruptly, I'd taken a cab back to Grigor's, barged in on him, and announced my intent to leave.

"I can't be part of anything where people are hurt," I told him.

He laughed at me. "Murder doesn't hurt? Beating people, breaking bones, selling them drugs? None of that hurts? Huh? The gun I sell that someone uses to kill his rival? That doesn't hurt? My God, what a hypocrite you are!"

I put up my hands, giving up on trying to get him to see it my way, and then charged toward the door.

"Wait!" he thundered, which froze me there with my hand on the doorknob. "Look at me."

I turned to him.

"Explain yourself."

I shrugged. "It's like, if you had to kill the cow, would you still eat burgers?"

He squinted at me. "What are you talking about?"

"It's the devil you see," I tried to explain. "I can't look at those women and know that I'm helping to hurt them."

"But the guns and the drugs and—"

"It's not *logical*," I conceded with a sigh. "I know that. But I can't help how I feel and I can't have those women—or those boys—looking at me like I could save them but I don't. I'm not made that way."

He stared at me and I met his gaze, holding it.

"Fine."

I was surprised. "Sorry?"

He waved a dismissive hand at me.

"Grigor?"

"I'm saying I agree," he said from behind his massive desk. "It's a lot of trouble, and I have too many women in my life to have to explain that to."

I stood there, gripping the doorknob to his study, overwhelmed not only by being listened to, but heeded.

"Come here, sit down. Let's talk about how to go about dismantling that piece of the business."

It was far easier than expected. Some girls got shipped home, others became strippers, dancers, hostesses, but everyone got on board with the change except Gennadi Maksimov. Gen, as everyone called him, had been one of the guys Grigor inherited when he took over from the last boss of the territory. Maksimov had thought that if he was simply insistent, Grigor would listen to reason.

I went to see him, and I took Marko with me.

We stood in his living room with the fireplace at our back, looking at Maksimov and his seven men. They were ready to kill us and start an open war with Grigor. Marko was hungover beside me, squinting from behind his aviators, and I was trying to think of a way to get through to Maksimov without having to kill all his men and leave him vulnerable. Salvation came when his wife walked through the kitchen, shopping bags hanging from hands dripping in diamonds and gold, perfectly french manicured.

"Mrs. Maksimov," I called out.

She turned to look at me.

"Will you please tell your husband that I don't want to take money away from him; I just don't want him to traffic in whores anymore."

"Shut your mouth," Maksimov snarled at me as he stood up.

She hissed something in Serbian and moved to the back of the couch, staring at me.

"I don't want him to be a pimp, I want him to be a legitimate businessman," I continued. "I mean, why would he want whores around anyway?"

Her eyes narrowed as she did a slow pan to her husband.

I watched him flinch, saw the tightening of his face, the flattening of his eyes as he stared at his truly stunning wife. She'd been a model before they were married, I'd heard that much, and unlike many other couples, they'd been together more than twenty years. She owned half of his whole world, and now I'd planted a seed of doubt.

He turned to look at me. "Meet me at the club first thing tomorrow morning."

I smiled at him. "Yessir."

Grigor was stunned when Marko and I came back without having fired our guns.

"How?"

"This one," Marko answered, tipping his head at me. "So clever."

I waggled my eyebrows at Grigor.

"It's why I hired him…"

"*Ceaton*?" Grigor's voice cracking brought me back to the present. "Sonya was taken, wasn't she."

"Grigor—"

"Ceaton!"

"Yes," I whispered.

There was a long moment of silence. "She's gone, right?"

"I'll find her."

"You"—I heard the tears right there on the surface—"won't find her. You'll find what's left."

"That's what I think," I agreed.

"I'll be here," he said softly.

"Okay," I answered and hung up.

I thought about Beron then, and whoever else had hurt Sonya, and wondered if they'd laughed at her when she told them that they'd die screaming once her cousin found out what happened to her. They'd had no idea they were killing a prophet.

WHEN GEARY finally returned my call early that evening, he told me that the police had gone to Carnal and were shown a video of a drunk, barely able to walk Sonya leaving the club with Ellen, who was in much the same condition. There were no cameras outside, but the police immediately came to the conclusion that neither woman was abducted. They had walked out under their own power and were probably sleeping it off somewhere, too embarrassed to tell their respective families. They were certain both would turn up.

"You need to bring the club owner in and question him," I told Geary as I checked my gun, watching Marko, Pravi, and Luka holster theirs, getting ready to go to Carnal ourselves. All roads led there, just as we knew they did; we simply needed to be more persuasive than the police were able to be.

"We've done all we can, Mr. Mercer. Clearly, Ms. Crncevic left the club in one piece. We just have to put together where she went after that. We're calling all the cab companies, and we're looking at the Metro and even Uber. We will find them."

I wasn't holding my breath.

We were on our way to the club when I got another call from Geary. It had barely been half an hour.

"Mr. Mercer," he sighed, sounding really old.

"Detective Geary," I replied, knowing already, feeling it, yet still holding my breath. The others stopped moving, all looking at me.

He cleared his throat. "Ms. Crncevic and Ms. Campbell have been identified."

Not found. *Identified*. Big difference. "Yes."

"They were discovered this morning in a landfill close to Mission Hill. The IDs just came in through the database. We're very sorry."

"And?"

"I don't—"

"How long?"

"How long what? How long has she been dead?"

I grunted.

"On site the medical examiner guessed maybe three days."

I absorbed that. "Where is she now?"

"With the M.E.," he said quietly. "You'll need to go down there to—"

"Got it," I said and hung up.

I shook my head at the guys. Pravi and Luka flopped down onto the couch, and Marko walked to the window and looked over the city while I called Grigor.

"Ceaton?"

"I'm so sorry, Grigor; she was gone before we even got on the plane."

Silence on his end.

"I'll find out everything." I assured him gruffly, my own voice dark and grainy. She'd been a sweet girl, feisty but kind, and I would miss her in Grigor's life. She'd been a light in the darkness that was him. Her influence had been good.

"Yes," he croaked.

"We'll find the men responsible."

He coughed. "Jaja will want an eye for an eye."

"Of course," I assured him because I knew he wasn't just talking about his aunt. He was the one who wanted everyone involved dead, and he wanted proof to show Jaja. "I'll call with status."

"You should get in touch with Sonya's friend's family and let them know what happened."

"I will," I sighed, dreading that.

"Ceaton."

I waited.

"I'm glad you're there. I'm glad it was you who called."

"I'll take care of it."

"I know," he said, his voice cracking.

"Lemme talk to Doran."

"Hold on."

There was a muffled sound and then, "Hey."

"Don't let him go anywhere without you, period."

"All right."

"I don't care what you have to say or do or—just don't. Tell him I said so, if he gets up in your face."

"You know I have been with him longer than you, yes?"

"Who's here, Dor, and who's there?"

"Fuck you, Ceaton."

"Listen, I—"

Marko grabbed the phone from me. "Doran Loncar," he snarled, using the man's full name, "anything happens to Grigor after Ceaton asks you to look after him, and you and I will have talk when I get home."

He listened for a moment.

"*Da*. I like him better," he finished simply and then passed me back my phone. "He will look out for Grigor as you asked."

"Thanks."

He gave a quick head tilt, telling me he'd heard, and then he pivoted and was heading for the door. I took a breath, wondering when we would see the suite again.

The trip to the morgue seemed like it took forever. Just walking up the front steps and then taking the elevator to the basement was bone-numbing.

I alone stepped through the door to meet the medical examiner, Gi Thomas. She was a lovely woman, tall and slender with delicate, fine features and a firm handshake. But mostly what I noticed was her deep, dark eyes filled with clear sorrow. "Mr. Mercer?"

I nodded. She led the way to a gurney and moved back the sheet, enough for me to see Sonya's sweet face. "Yeah, that's her."

"Okay," Thomas sighed and replaced the covering, then looked at me, unsure. I should have been leaving, but I wasn't.

"I need to know what happened," I told her, my voice steady and low.

She took a breath. "I'll have a report compiled for—"

"Please," I coaxed gently. "It's imperative I know." It was. I had to be aware so I'd know what punishment to dish out when I found those responsible. "Was she raped?"

Thomas shook her head. "Normally when we find these girls, bruised, covered in blood, covered in needle marks, they've been sexually assaulted. But your girl—she must have been a real fighter."

"How so?"

"There are defensive wounds all over her face and body, and there's more than just tissue under her fingernails, there's blood too."

"So she put up a helluva fight."

"Yes," Thomas said, nodding. "And though I don't know for sure, I suspect that in her all-out effort to get free, someone hit her too hard or—something."

"They literally broke her," I said flatly.

"Yes," she agreed solemnly. "The evidence points that way."

"What killed her?"

"Her neck was wrenched sideways and snapped."

I nodded.

"Why would you want me to tell you these things? No one needs to hear these kinds of horrific details, Mr. Mercer."

I met her gaze. "You do for specific reasons, Dr. Thomas."

She took a breath. "I don't think I want to know."

"It's probably for the best."

I was turning to go, but she reached out, offering me her hand, and I took it in both of mine.

"I will care for her here, Mr. Mercer."

"Thank you. Arrangements are being made to take her home."

She nodded.

"How was she found?"

"Naked and wrapped in a tarp."

"Thrown out like garbage."

"Again, you have my sincerest condolences on your loss."

I squeezed her hand one last time and was at the door when she stopped me again.

"Pardon my frankness, Mr. Mercer, but you don't seem angry or terribly sad but more—resigned. Am I reading that right?"

"Yes, ma'am."

"I'm sorry. I don't meet many avenging angels in my line of work."

"Not an angel," I assured her. "Definitely not that."

"I think like many things, it's in the eye of the beholder."

I'd found that to be true over the years as well.

When I'd become a Marine, I had thought I would be helping the world, doing good, changing lives, but there was no way to actually make significant change as I was a single person. Even as part of a platoon or bigger formation, with as many men as we had, once we left a place, it was either worse off or somewhat better, but the effect, I'd found, for me, was minimal. The thing was, working for Grigor, was a little bit of the same. I pulled one weed; another grew right back up in its place. The difference was that sometimes, if I dug down deep enough and burned all the roots, the whole thing stayed dead.

I suspected we would be in Boston until every little scrap of the machine that had turned its filthy eye on Sonya was eviscerated. We would start at the beginning.

THE POLICE couldn't do anything else without evidence pointing to someone, but for us, again, all roads led back to Beron, the owner of Carnal. It turned out it had been easy for him to lie to the police. Not so easy to lie to me, Marko, Luka, and Pravi.

We parked across the street from the club. It was late Monday night now, so we waited until it emptied, bided our time until the men who were there with Beron had drinks and more drinks and had sex with the girls still there in the back rooms and then finally after two in the morning, came staggering out. And only when the whole place was cleared and Beron left with his three bodyguards, did we move, trailing him for a half a mile before Pravi grunted.

"Yeah?" I asked from the passenger seat.

"*Da*," he agreed, nodding at the industrial area we were passing. "This is good."

We pulled our guns as he stamped on the gas pedal. The rented Chevy Suburban flew forward as Pravi whipped us around in front of them and braked hard, cutting them off, forcing them to a bouncing, screeching stop. There was no time to get their bearings before Marko was out of the SUV.

He shot the driver and the passenger fast—one two, bam-bam, that quick, no giant blast of a machine gun, no Hollywood spray of bullets, just done. He didn't fuck around. And when Beron and another guy in the back got out, Pravi took out the man we didn't give a shit about as I put Beron in my sights.

"You don't know who you're fucking with!" he screamed at me in heavily Russian-accented English.

"Actually, I do," I apprised him. "Sadly, it was *you* who had no idea who you were fucking with. Or should I say, whose girl you were fucking with."

He was scared but also confused.

"Don't worry," I said as Marko reached him and took his gun. "I'll explain."

At the nearby deserted warehouse Luka drove us to, I got the spiel again.

"I don't know who the fuck you think you are, but I'm Kostya Beron!"

"Like that means shit to me," I said, squatting down so we were at eye level. I wasn't a giant, but at six two, I always had to kneel when I had conversations with people tied to chairs.

When he saw me, really took in my bored expression, the heavy muscles, the width of my shoulders and the size of my hands, the whole story came spilling out. Yes, Sonya and Ellen had left under their own power, but they only got as far as the curb. They thought they'd gotten away, but the women had been drugged out of their minds. Beron's men collected them on the sidewalk and put them in a car.

"Where'd they go from there?" I asked him softly, gently.

"I don't know. Sergei handles the girls."

"Sergei who?" I prodded patiently.

"Fuck you," he retorted, trying to sound fierce, trying to spit at me, but he was too scared so there was no saliva to spare. I'd been there; I knew what it was like. Being terrified made your mouth dry, so he ended up retching instead.

Marko passed me a knife—he didn't have to, I carried my own, but seeing him do it gave Beron time to find his voice.

He gave up the name Sergei Utkin.

It was enough. The name gave us our next step and was, in fact, all Beron knew. And since there couldn't be a trail—that was just logical— there was nothing else to be done but clean up.

While pulling my gun and screwing on the silencer, I was not surprised when Beron started to cry. In my experience all badass criminals broke down at the end. It was the epiphany of imminent death—all the unfinished business—and the feeling of utter powerlessness. How many people had this man murdered, butchered, thrown away like nothing?

And now, here was his karmic justice, and all his sins would transfer to me. Because I didn't get off; my own soul had been put up for collateral after the first man I killed in this life I'd chosen.

"Enough," Marko grumbled.

I turned to look at him as he kicked Beron's chair over and shot him in the head. It was messy, but the spray gushed away from us, not on our clothes. I'd made that mistake quite a bit in the beginning. It was fast, no suffering, the fall had been the most jarring part of it.

"What's wrong with you?"

"You," he huffed. "You make this so depressing."

I crossed my arms, still holding my gun. "Oh?"

"Yes," he groused, almost whining. "Always you berate yourself, every single time, and you think, one more death on my head, but Ceaton… if they were good men, why would we ever see them?"

There was that.

"Why would I be here, or you or Pravi or Luka?"

"You do get really moody after," Luka chimed in.

"Is that right?" I asked, deadpan.

He shrugged.

"It's a good thing," Pravi added.

Marko shot him a look.

"No, I mean, it's a good thing he's not a psychopath, right?"

"I am not so convinced," Marko concluded.

Pravi groaned.

"I think it's a good thing that you don't want to kill everyone," Luka clarified, indicating all of us. "But I also think you shouldn't take this all on yourself, like the second you die you are going to hell or something. Because if everything is God's plan, aren't you part of that as well?"

"No, no, no," Marko said, stepping in close to me, hand on my shoulder. "We are all going to hell, make no mistake. We kill people, we all go to church, we are not stupid men. We all know how it will be."

"I don't go to church," I chimed in.

"See, that is sin as well," Marko passed judgment.

"Now I'm depressed," Pravi teased.

"But what is hell?" Marko asked. "Some place you never leave, where all your friends are?" He shrugged. "So really, how bad can this be?"

I glanced around at the men I spent all my time with. "So you're saying lighten up?"

Marko clapped me on the back. "*Da*."

"Okay, then," I said, exhaling, letting the tension drain out of me. "I'll try and not let all the murder get me down."

"*Dobro*," Pravi said, chuckling.

"Don't start with the Serbian," I warned him.

"You need to learn it, like I did," Marko groused, walking over to the gasoline can he'd brought in with us and then returning to pour it over the body of Kostya Beron. He didn't carry a lighter. He didn't believe in lighting his cigarettes or cigars with butane, only wooden matches. Something about the flavor. Those wooden matches had come in handy many times over the years.

As we walked away, I heard first the strike of the match on the side of the box and then the whoosh of flame behind us. Like Marko, I was a fan of setting things on fire. It was hard to pull DNA evidence from charred anything, no matter what they said on TV.

"Let's go back to his place," I suggested.

Everyone was in agreement.

So we returned to Carnal. After a thorough walk-through, making sure no one was there sleeping off a hangover, I emptied bottles of booze all over the furniture as Marko made Molotov cocktails and lined them up on the bar.

Pravi went into the back office and brought out some chairs that he kicked apart to make kindling, and Luka hacked into the video surveillance so he could make a copy of the video of Sonya walking out of the bar. He uploaded it to Grigor's iCloud so our boss could see it and then loaded a virus onto their VPN—that would be the cherry on the cake of Utkin's day of losing first Beron and then this club.

It had to go. There was no way we could leave the spiderweb up for another mother's little butterfly to wander into, never to be seen again. And once it was fully engulfed in flames, burning fast and hot, I had a feeling of closure. This way we sent the police a message too—you should have been watching this place.

WE CHANGED hotels. Not that the place wasn't perfect, but things were going to explode, so we needed to be able to move quickly and quietly. And being stuck at the top of a high rise was great for a sniper, not so great for anyone else. Plus we needed to pay with cash. But the point was to make it look like we'd checked in somewhere and then had departed. The paper trail was important.

As far as Boston PD knew, we'd left the day before Beron's club burned to the ground and so had nothing to do with that incident. When they checked, we'd chartered a private jet home to Vegas. But they had no way of knowing that only Sonya's body was making the return trip, along with Doran, who'd come on the plane only to turn right back around and go home again. He asked me to let him stay and send Luka home in his place, but Luka was my guy—Doran had always been Grigor's. Even contemplating it had felt wrong.

"That was good choice," Marko told me as we drove away from the airport. "You have to have the men you know."

I nodded as I took the left back out onto the highway. "You know I trust all of you with my life. You're stuck with me now."

It took me a few minutes to realize no one was talking, and I finally stopped keeping track of where Google Maps was telling me to go and glanced sideways at Marko.

"What?"

He shook his head.

I checked the rearview mirror and saw Pravi behind me, looking out his window. When I looked at Luka, his eyes were down, something on his phone utterly riveting.

"The hell?" I growled at all of them.

"*Jebi se*," Pravi snarled, punching the back of my seat. "Fuck you, C."

"For crissakes, man, you're gonna make me wreck!" I yelled.

"Then do not say such shit," Marko griped, smacking my chest with his big paw of a hand. "None of that needs to be said. We would follow—it does not matter."

They were both really mad. That made no sense.

"You don't have to say things like that," Luka explained after a moment of quiet. "We're—the four of us—this is done."

"Yeah, but Grigor could—"

"No," Marko husked, not turning his head, never looking at me. "Things are different since you came."

"How?"

"Grigor trusts you," Pravi answered from behind me. "Grigor gives you things to do, all the dirt he no longer wants to touch."

That was true.

"You remember when we saw him at dinner at Scarpetta with the people from the casino?" Luka reminded me.

"Yeah."

"And he didn't even get up to say hello."

"Oh come on," I countered. "What would he tell those people? These are the guys that kill people for me?"

"No," Marko whispered, still not looking at me. "But he could excuse himself and meet us at the bar."

He could have, yes.

Luka cleared his throat. "You were on that date with the flight attendant, and you took him to Jardin."

"I did."

"And then after, you were walking through the Wynn, and Pravi and I were there."

"I know, asshole. I brought him over to meet you guys."

"*Yes*," Luka agreed. "You *did*."

I wasn't sure why that was important.

"You chose to meet my brother when he flew through Vegas," Marko ground out.

"Yeah, he said like two whole words to me."

He coughed. "I asked Grigor to go, just to say hello."

"No, I know, but he was—"

"You were the busy one," he told me. "But you made time."

I had always thought Marko was terrifying, but holy crap had I been wrong. His brother—who'd been killed in a shootout since then—was twice as big with scars on his face that should have left him eyeless. I'd never seen a scarier-looking man. He was a Bond villain—the man was that much larger than life—but now I knew… that effort had been important. Had meant more than Marko had ever let on.

He was still turned away. In fact, they all were, all three of them, eyes turned to look outside, none on me.

"Who wants to eat?"

They were all ready for lunch.

We never spoke about us being family again. Not that we really had that time, but still, I got the picture. It felt like when I was in the Corps, when things were good, and the pocket of cold that was leftover inside, from being abandoned, from being discarded, got filled up by the regard of those three men. And there was Grigor, of course, but that became peripheral, and that was okay too. It didn't matter. He kept us together, and that was his role even as he distanced himself from us.

But that day in Boston, I got it. And after lunch when we went to the cheap motel and waited, making ourselves sitting ducks, I felt better than I had in almost two years.

"I think we should bowl."

We all turned to look at Luka.

"What?"

"Bowl?" Pravi asked him from where he reclined on one of the twin beds, stretched out with his gun and silencer in his lap.

"Yeah," Luka told him. "It's supposed to be a great no-pressure way to meet women."

Marko, who was leaning on the doorframe of the bathroom, scowled at him. "You want we should wear stupid shirts."

"I want you to bowl, *kurac*, and try not to scare the shit outta everyone."

He shook his head like Luka was an idiot.

"C?"

"I'll bowl," I told him. "But I'm getting my own shoes. Renting them is gross."

Marko pointed at me. "*Da*. We buy."

Pravi rolled his eyes as we all heard a car pull into the driveway.

"I think I need a bulletproof vest," Luka announced. "It would make my mother feel better."

I groaned and so did Pravi, but Marko said yes, for Mrs. Novak, he'd get him one.

"Excellent," Luka chirped happily, drawing his gun.

The guy who kicked down the front door and the guy who came around the back were dead in both doorways in seconds. The good news was that the motel was so crappy that no one heard a thing, and being on the first floor, the bodies were easy to load into the back of the SUV. The bad news was that after the shooting, we had only one guy to talk to about Utkin, and he flipped on his boss much too fast. Marko didn't even have to get out his gear, his pliers or knives; the guy just told us what we wanted to know with a gun shoved in his face.

"Disappointing," Marko grumbled, closing the rear hatch on the Suburban after loading up the guy who'd spilled his guts. Literally. Again, there could never be loose ends. "What kind of man allows a Glock to frighten him?"

"Listen," I answered with a sigh. "Not everyone is ex-Russian Special Forces, right?"

He glanced back at me over his shoulder. "I know men with no military training who are not afraid of one small gun."

"Yeah, but really, how many?" I said, grinning at him. "Most guys piss their pants."

I got a rare smile, the one that put a spark in the inky darkness of his eyes. He was one of the scariest men I knew, and I was really glad to call him friend.

"Hey," I offered cheerfully. "Maybe you'll get to torture someone later."

His grunt told me he was not all that hopeful.

IT TURNED out that Marko did get to break some bones with the next set of men, and after three of his crew died howling in front of him, Utkin gave up *his* boss, Feliks Volkov.

"See," I said to Marko as he rolled up the two dead, along with the sledgehammer he'd used, in plastic. "You had more fun that time."

He didn't look happy. Of course Utkin, who was duct taped to a chair, appeared far less pleased than my irritated friend.

I called Grigor as Luka sat in a chair at his laptop, bitching about the cold, and Pravi sloshed gasoline around yet another abandoned warehouse.

"Ceaton," he greeted me.

"We have a new name that I think is as high as this goes here."

"Good. Wait for me, then. Do nothing more until I arrive."

"The fuck are you coming here for?" That made no sense.

"You know why."

He liked to watch people get what was coming to them, and as a boss to a boss, he wanted to watch Volkov die. Never let it be said that Grigor Jankovic was any less bloodthirsty than Marko Borodin.

"It's too risky. The police are looking into the murders, and when this warehouse goes up, they'll know what's going on, for sure. The only thing that connects these men is Sonya."

"You think the police have made these connections?"

"Of course. This is their town; they know what's going on. And nobody's this stupid. They'll know it's a vendetta."

"And you think they'll suspect me?"

"You through us, sure. We're the thing that was different, and we came for you and your family. The detective, Geary, he knows that too."

"He doesn't know you're still there."

"He wouldn't have to look too hard. He just hasn't yet."

Grigor was quiet, contemplating that I was guessing.

"I'm still coming. I'll take a commercial flight and fly under my alias."

"Is there anything I can say to dissuade you?"

"No. I need to look this man in the eye."

"Okay, then, we'll wait."

"Good. I'll text you the flight number."

The time-out gave me time to talk to Ellen's family, the Campbells, who were sweet people from the Midwest with a farm and a small online business that shipped cinnamon apple butter and orchard-scented candles all over the US. The police had contacted them, and I found out Ellen's brother Harper was there in Boston, too, trying to get answers. When I went to meet him with Marko in tow, at a diner in Beacon Hill, he was thrilled to meet us.

When I took a seat across from him, my first thought was that he was certainly attractive. I normally didn't notice what people looked like when I was working, but he reminded me of the algebra teacher from tenth grade I'd had a crush on. Harper looked gentle and bookish and sweet. He was handsome in that way that could grow on you over time, not the traffic-stopping kind that Pravi was. It rattled me a little, that I noticed him, because I shouldn't have.

What it also told me was that I badly needed to get laid when I got home.

"Hey," I greeted him, smiling, trying to look as nonthreatening as possible. Between the overcoat and the width of my shoulders, it wasn't always possible.

Marko grabbed the chair to my right so he could see the door and the front windows at the same time, and I noticed how Harper glanced at Marko once and then again quickly. He inhaled sharply through his nose, and for a second, I thought he was scared—until I saw his lips part and then the slight tremor that ran through him.

In the midst of the horror visited on him, he was reacting viscerally to Marko. I understood, I did. It was like seeing a tiger up close; you were terrified and excited at the same time. Plus, if you were looking to feel safe and could see past his scary outer shell, Marko Borodin was the guy you wanted watching over you.

"So," I said to Harper once he could finally tear his eyes away from Marko. "I'm very sorry about your sister."

"Thank you," he said sadly, the ache and weariness of living through the death of a loved one clinging to him like a shroud.

"Were they close, Ellen and Sonya?"

He nodded. "Yeah, they were friends all through college."

"That's nice," I said lamely.

"You know, the only reason Sonya was even in Boston was to help El get settled."

I knew that. Sonya had flown in to spend time with Ellen before she herself moved to San Francisco to take a job at a magazine. I just hadn't known the extent of the friendship. I hoped they had been some comfort to each other in their final moments.

"I mean—maybe Sonya would still be alive if she hadn't come here to help El."

"No," I said adamantly, reaching out, taking hold of his shoulder, squeezing tight, needing him to hear me. "They're dead because they crossed paths with bad men."

"I—"

"That is all," I assured him.

He glanced at Marko, whose scowl and quick tip of his head made it clear he agreed. "Your sister and Grigor's cousin, they were prey. You understand?"

Harper nodded before turning back to me.

"Any blame you feel or your family feels, get rid of that," I told him, letting go of him, leaning back in my chair. "It's crap. These were young women living their lives, nothing more."

"Okay," he said as tears seeped from his eyes.

"Really," I insisted. "Their actions—those men responsible—they are the only ones that matter."

He inhaled shakily. "I'm taking Ellen's body home," he explained, absolutely broken.

"Good."

He lifted his head to meet my gaze. "Are you a religious man?"

"I'm not," I answered him solemnly. "I've seen too many things for God to make sense."

"I am," he said after a moment.

"That's good," I assured him. "That'll be a comfort for you, then."

"It's not, though," he explained. "I've gone to church, I've talked to a priest—to several, actually—and they all say the same thing, that she's with God now, that I should be happy, that she's safe and at rest."

"This is shit," Marko muttered, leaning in to look Harper in the eye. "There is no comfort for you but justice."

"Yes," Harper breathed, his eyes full of Marko before glancing at me.

"You look like a man who has a question," I said because it was obvious.

He continued to stare at me. "Sonya always alluded to the fact that her cousin was a dangerous man who had scary men working for him."

I remained still, not wanting to interrupt.

"Her cousin," he began haltingly, "he won't wait for God to punish the men who killed Sonya, will he?"

"What makes you say that?"

"Sonya led us to believe, my sister and me and our parents, that her cousin Grigor was the kind of man who took matters into his own hands."

"*Da*," Marko answered, sounding bored.

"He is," I agreed.

"So that's a yes, then. He won't wait for God."

Normally I wouldn't say anything because that could incriminate me and Marko as well as Grigor. But Harper was grieving, and so was his family, which made the worry over being careful moot. "No," I answered, my voice severe.

"And it won't just be vengeance for Sonya."

I shook my head. "No. It'll be for Ellen too."

"Really?"

"Of course," I admitted stoically. "You have to think, if something had happened to Ellen and Sonya found out, then who would she have called to get justice for her friend?"

"Yeah, okay. That makes sense."

"What are you trying to ask me?"

He cleared his throat. "Will he… will Grigor… will he… hurt—" He took a breath. "Will you hurt those men?"

"We will kill those men," Marko told him flat out. "We have already started."

No catch of breath, no gasp of outrage or alarm. Harper just turned his pretty gray eyes back to me. "I… if I could… if you'd let me… I'd like to see what happens to the men who killed my sister."

"You want to watch?"

"If I can."

"Are you certain?"

His dead eyes were locked on mine. "I am."

I had to take him at his word, but still. "You can never forget if you see."

"I had to identify the body in the morgue," he replied simply. "I don't mind having something else in my head to cancel that out."

I understood.

So the following day, all of us, including Grigor and Ellen's sweet brother Harper, went to talk to Feliks Volkov.

It shouldn't have been so easy to get to him, to breach the defenses of his mansion and walk in through the front door. Never mind that we were ridiculously well-armed, that I had been a sniper, and it was easy to pick off men from the abandoned house across the street, or that Pravi and Luka, covered in Kevlar, mowed down anything that moved, or that Doran, who'd come back to Boston with Grigor, was freakishly gifted with knives—the throwing kind, hunting, military issue—and carved up everyone in the house but the maid, whom he locked in the broom closet.

Marko had gone around the side and made the men walking the perimeter put the dogs back in the kennels before he killed them. The men, of course. Not the dogs. He had a soft spot for all four-legged creatures. When he leaned around the side of the house, waving both arms at me, giving me the all-clear, I called his cell.

"There is no one else back here," he reported.

"Yeah, I think we're good in the front too."

He tsked. "This is disappointing."

I knew it was. It should have been more of a fight, should have been harder for us, easily thirty of them against seven of us, counting Marko and Grigor and also Harper, who sat quietly beside me with binoculars and kept a running tally of the dead. But as it turned out, I'd played harder levels on *Call of Duty*.

I had to give Volkov credit for not cowering in the corner when we walked into the den of his home, what should have been his safe place. Instead he stood by the fireplace, arm on the mantel, sipping bourbon. It would have been more impressive if the ice hadn't clinked against the side of the glass with the shaking of his hand. But still, I had to give it to him.

"Who will come after me when you're dead?" Grigor asked. It was always good to get as much information from the mark as you could.

Volkov threatened him then, explained that his boss in St. Petersburg would kill not only him, but his entire family.

"It's lucky, then, that all the family I have is all you see here," Grigor lied with an added scoff rife with derision.

"You're all going to die," Volkov swore, sounding less like a man and more like a wounded animal.

"Why Sonya?" Grigor wanted to know. "Why Ellen?"

And the answer, coming only after Marko took the man's eyes, was simple. The girls had been there. It was a crime of convenience.

Harper puked, but he just wiped his mouth when he was done and kept standing beside Grigor.

"Did she tell you that you would die screaming?" Grigor wanted to know.

"She did," Volkov admitted before Marko cut out his tongue.

"You should have listened to her," was the last thing Grigor said.

I didn't stay to the end. I didn't need to. Even though Volkov was still breathing, he wouldn't be for long. So I was already outside when Marko drenched him in gasoline and Grigor set him on fire. The final act was just the screaming, until that, too, finally subsided. Grigor taped the whole thing for Aunt Jaja and put the man's eyes in a Ziploc that he would hand deliver to her when he returned home. Harper was allowed to take some pictures, five total, and they could only stay on his phone, no backing them up anywhere. Grigor trusted him—they were brothers in their grief now—and so did I. He was a sweet guy who'd been sent to hell for a day. I worried about how it would affect him long-term, but I wasn't concerned that he'd ever turn on any of us. We were divine bringers of justice, and he loved us for it.

"I have to go back to the hotel and call Jaja," Grigor told me as I stood beside his car. Doran was already behind the wheel, having squeezed my arm before he got in. As a rule we weren't close, but the two days had been strange, and like me, I was sure, he felt untethered. Anything familiar was good.

"Just to tell her it's over?"

"No. She'll want all the details."

"But what purpose does that serve?" I asked. "Why would she want to hear the entire timeline of her daughter's death from beginning to end?" It felt masochistic to me.

"So she can understand precisely what happened to her child and when."

My throat went dry, and my stomach knotted just thinking about the animals that hurt Jaja's little bird. Even though they were all dead now, still, it would gut Jaja to know the specifics.

"And she'll do what, think about Sonya calling for her, wanting her mother right before she died? I can't—that's horrible."

"It's what Jaja needs to know."

"Just make sure she sees the video too, right? All of it. Show her how that guy died howling over how sorry he was."

"I will. You know I will."

"Maybe when she knows everything… maybe then she'll be able to grieve."

"She will," he whispered. "Closure is healing."

"I hope so," I conceded, turning to leave.

He stopped me with a hand around my bicep, making sure I couldn't pull away from him.

"Grigor?"

"You and the others," he murmured, letting go of me only to slide his hand up to my shoulder and take hold. "When you are done cleaning up, come to the Hyatt and stay in the suite with me and Doran. I don't want you in that shithole anymore."

"It's safer," I assured him.

He shrugged. "If they ask, if anyone asks, I came to see the city my cousin died in and my men came with me."

"You don't think that'll look a little suspicious?"

"I don't think anyone will have the balls to question me since they failed to protect her or find her until it was too late."

"Grigor—"

"Fine," he snapped, his hand on the side of my neck. "Leave the others there, but you—you I want there with me. You're the only one I can talk to."

But we didn't normally talk. That I did with Pravi and Luka, and Marko. Grigor and I just sat, a lot of times in silence, and it was that, truth be told, that he liked the best. Not having to fill every moment with conversation was a blessing in and of itself.

"Okay," I agreed, smiling at him, leaning forward, into him, giving him the hug he opened for, welcomed. "We'll drop Harper off, finish the cleanup, and go get our stuff."

"Good," he said gruffly, wiping his face on my shoulder, tears there that I saw, that he wouldn't allow anyone else to see.

When I returned to the others, I announced the plan and Marko made a noise that was halfway between a grunt and a tsk, not complimentary, mostly judgmental.

"What?"

"He wants you with him, but you will not go without us, so now the offer includes us all."

"You're wrong."

"I seldom am," he assured me, before indicating Harper with an open hand.

"What?"

"I think he will pass out."

And Marko was right, as he often was.

Harper, who was following Pravi, wobbled for a second, giving me just enough time to reach him before his head fell back and he sagged toward the ground. He passed out cold in my arms.

"Newbies," Luka joked, and we all remembered the last time *he* had passed out—when Marko went to work on a guy with a blowtorch.

I got Harper situated in the car, putting him between me and Pravi in the backseat. Luka drove, and when we reached Harper's hotel, he parked the car and let me and Marko out. At the front desk, I explained that the stag party got crazy and that our buddy was sloshed.

"Ohmygod, he's hammered," the cute clerk tittered, clearly amused by Harper's condition. "And look at you, all big and strong and carrying him around like he's nothing."

I gave her a grin and an arched eyebrow. "Could you just tell me what room he's in, sweetie? I have the key card, I just don't know where to dump him."

More giggling and she gave me the room number—and wrote down her phone number for me, on a sticky note.

In the elevator, Marko grunted.

"What?"

"Women love you. They miss that you are gay."

Some did, some didn't, but he was right: I got hit on a lot by women, men too. My problem wasn't finding people interested in me, but finding people who I was interested in back, and for more than one night. Really, with my job, a relationship was a ridiculous dream. I understood how it could work for Grigor and other guys at his level, but I had no idea how it was supposed to even be possible at mine.

"I don't wear a sign, jackass," I groused at Marko, irritated by my situation, not by him.

Second grunt. "Perhaps you should."

He was just foul. He hadn't killed nearly enough people on this trip. At home we could always find something—it was Vegas, after all—but here, it was a bit of a drought.

In the hotel room, Marko used the bathroom to clean up the blood that had been hidden by his gloves and suit jacket while I dumped Harper in the bed.

I stripped him down to his boxers, took everything—jacket, polo, jeans, socks, his now soot-covered white Converse sneakers, all of it—and put it in one of the plastic bags that were supposed to be used for laundry. He hadn't been close enough to get any blood trace on him, but still, better to be safe than sorry. I got him under the covers, closed the curtains, turned off the lights, and after checking his plane ticket, called down to the concierge to set up a wake-up call for him for the morning.

On my way out, his voice stopped me.

"Thank you for everything."

"You're welcome."

"I hope I never see you again for the rest of my life."

"Me too," I agreed gently, closing the door behind me, his clothes in hand.

Marko was waiting for me.

"Oh, you look better," I commented, indicating the T-shirt he had on under the suit jacket. "Very urban."

He flipped me off, and we headed back down to the lobby together.

THE BROTHEL was the last piece of the whole mess and had to be handled. So before we met up with Grigor later that night, we went to the place where Sonya and Ellen had been taken. It turned out to be nothing like the ones Grigor used to run in Vegas, instead simply two stories of a house in a shitty neighborhood in East Boston. We could have left it alone, but like Beron's club, Carnal, it had to be handled. Not only was it a loose end, but having made his decision about the sex trade for himself and his business, Grigor wouldn't allow the brothel Sonya was killed in to continue. Had it been a true brothel, the kind where women—and men—were there of their own free will, he might have left it alone. But the point was, none of it had ever been set up with anyone's permission; there had only ever been victims, never willing participants. For those reasons, and most of all because of the threat of rape that existed there, and least of all because Jaja needed closure, we were there to raze it to the ground.

After quickly shooting our way in, we gathered all the men in the downstairs living room, put them on their knees, hands behind their backs, and gagged them with scarves, pillow cases, socks, just whatever we could find. Then we brought in the girls—dressed, no longer nude or in lingerie—as a group. One by one I stood behind each man and asked the girls yes or no.

They understood even though most of them spoke different languages than me as well as each other.

After I killed the first two, the third guy wet himself. I was ready to pull the trigger, but it turned out he was okay. All the girls shook their heads over him, waved their hands at me and said no. He was good. He fed them. He insisted the bathroom be fixed so they didn't have to piss in a bucket, and he made sure there were always condoms, and he let them shower. I lifted him up off the ground, and even though he was shaking and crying—and covered in urine—he grabbed my hand and kissed it.

"You never saw me, yeah?"

He nodded and ran from the house. I had no doubt he was running to tell whoever he knew what was happening, but everyone above him was dead already, so I wasn't all that worried. I executed fifteen men who had, as a group, raped and beaten every girl there. When I was done, I called 911, gave them the address, and told the girls help was coming.

First they wanted to go with us.

"You need to stay here. We're gonna send people to fix you all up," I promised even as two of them grabbed hold of each of my forearms. They'd just watched me commit cold-blooded murder, and still they wanted to stick to me like glue. "You don't need to be afraid anymore."

Then they wanted us to stay.

"We'll go to prison," I assured them.

Only then did they tell us to go.

We drove around the corner and watched from an alley as the police, EMTs, and a sea of other first responders showed up.

"Well done," Pravi told Luka and me as he draped an arm over Luka's shoulders and put a hand on my back. "Come on. Now we drink."

And we did. Too much. But not until after I'd stopped and set fire to Harper's clothes before we got to the hotel where we met Grigor. Loose ends, I really did hate them.

LATE THAT night, I was sitting in front of the window that looked out into downtown Boston when Pravi flopped down beside me. Marko was on the other side of me, asleep, and Luka was stretched out on the other couch. None of us had gone into one of the bedrooms to sleep, even Grigor, instead remaining clustered together in the common room of the suite.

"You look like you're contemplating the meaning of life," Pravi teased, whispering so he didn't wake the others.

I turned, slowly, to look at him. "Why do you think they never fight?"

"What are you talking about?"

"Like those guys tonight," I explained, shifting closer to him so we were shoulder to shoulder. "We put them on the floor and they just stayed there."

"What would you have had them do?"

"Fight."

"Fight how?"

"Like charge us, refuse to be put on their knees, something."

"To do what, die faster?"

"But see, that's my point. If you know you're gonna die anyway, why do it like that?"

"You make no sense."

"Yeah, I do," I argued, still a little buzzed by that time, but sobering up. "I mean, I get it if we had their families or something, and they were keeping still and doing what we said because they didn't want us to kill someone they loved, but to just sit there like sheep—I just don't get that," I finished while taking in the skyline.

I fell quiet, thinking, and when Marko moved, bumping me, stretching out so his thigh was plastered to mine, I turned to look at him. His eyes were slits, but he was awake.

"Self-preservation."

"What?" I asked quietly.

He swallowed before reaching for the bottle of water beside him on the end table. After draining it, his attention returned to me. "You asked why those men did as we said and did not fight us."

"Yeah."

He grunted.

"You're saying it was self-preservation."

"*Da.*"

"But they knew they were gonna die."

"Maybe. The longer it lasts, whatever it is, you have chance to get away. Like the man from the brothel you allowed to live. Had he fought, he would be dead. But tonight, he lives—we assume. Perhaps whoever is left in Volkov's organization shot him for running away when you let him. We do not know, we do not care. But the others, they thought—I will put off death for as long as I can. That is all."

"I just don't get that. If you know you're gonna die anyway, why not fight to your last breath? Why sit there and let me kill you?"

"I, too, would fight," he yawned. "But we are not sheep, we are men."

"It's too simple an answer."

"Or you are thinking too much."

"Maybe."

"Most people give up," Marko said before he closed his eyes. "This is not your way, so it does not occur to you."

I wondered about that too.

ON THE flight home on the chartered jet, Grigor announced we'd be returning to Boston. He'd decided to make it our new home.

"What?" I whined, in pain, hungover and as confused as everyone else.

"We have dismantled a large part of the Russians' business very quickly," he reminded us. "We should see what else we can do there."

"Really?" I whimpered, squinting at him from behind my aviators. Dammit, I knew better than to try to outdrink Marko even if it had been tequila instead of vodka.

"Yes, really," he said happily. "From out of this tragedy, we will find a new home. You'll see, it will be a good move for us."

I wasn't convinced, but I had no say in the matter. And so ready or not, like it or not, we were out of Vegas and moving to Boston.

CHAPTER THREE

THE CELL phone ringing woke me from a deep sleep. I was trained to do that, to go from passed out to alert in seconds, and it served me as well now as it did when I was serving my country. The ring was loud. I had no idea why until I remembered how deafening it was in the club the night before, and I came home and tumbled into bed without turning it down.

Rolling over on my back, I pulled the phone from the breast pocket of my suit jacket. "What?"

Snickering followed. "Nice."

"Fuck you," I growled at Aleksandar "Aca" Jankovic, my boss's annoying nephew, newly arrived from Las Vegas and tasked with learning the business. "The hell do you want?"

"Grigor said I could ask anyone to go on the run with me today, so I want you."

Normally I would have said something more to him before I hung up, but I was too tired and he was too annoying. Jesus, how stupid was he? Things like that, the run, were never discussed on the phone. And even if they were, the hell did he get off thinking I would go? When Grigor said he could take anyone, he meant certain guys, new guys, just muscle, nothing else. I would not have been included on that list.

When the phone rang again, I checked the number before answering. It was Aca again. I didn't pick up, and as that call rolled over to my voice mail, I checked the time—a little after one in the afternoon—and realized it was Sunday already. The weekends had been flying by lately. I really hoped Grigor would meet someone he liked again at some point soon so he'd spend Friday and Saturday nights holed up at her place fucking instead of going out and hitting the clubs until the wee hours of the morning. It was exhausting keeping up with him when all I wanted to do was stream shows on Netflix.

The third time the phone went off, I answered even though the number wasn't familiar. Sometimes Grigor called from wherever he was just to screw with the Feds and give them yet another number to add to the ever-growing list of those they were tapping. Like he didn't know they had everything bugged. They weren't exactly subtle with their unmarked surveillance vans or, lately, men in cars with government plates. Grigor had made a name for himself in Boston over the past three years, and although the police had absolutely nothing on him, they were always watching. It was ridiculous, which was why Aca's faux pas would need to be dealt with.

"Hello?"

"*Kako si*?" Came the words without a hint of an accent.

"Why're you hitting me with the Serbian when you know I just woke up?"

"You said to help, so I'm helping."

Fuck. "Okay, so what was that again?"

Snort of laughter before a command of "Think," from the other end.

I was tired, or it wouldn't have been hard. "Oh, you asked how I am."

"*Da*."

I had to get my brain to work and it was foggy at best. "Uhm, *dobro. A ti*?"

"Nice," he said with a chuckle. "You're improving."

"I'm trying." And I was. I had made it my goal, finally, after all this time, to master the language. I'd asked for serious help a week ago, and Pravi and Luka had really been trying to catch me up. "So what's going on?"

"I want to know—" Luka yawned. "—what happened to you last night."

"What're you talking about? You were with me last night."

"No, later, with the girl."

"Girl?"

"Yeah."

"What girl?" He'd lost me. "Why would there be a girl?"

"I know," he agreed with a scoff. "That's what I said to Marko, but he said you were making out with some blonde chick."

I groaned. "Why are you fucking with me when you know I'm hungover?"

"Listen, I thought I saw a girl all over you and then Marko said yeah, there was."

"When?"

"At the club."

"Oh, for crissakes, which one?"

He snorted out a laugh. "How much did you drink last night?"

It felt like gallons. "You were there."

"I saw the vodka shots and the beer. Was there more than that?"

"Apparently."

"Man, you need to slow down."

"Tell Grigor," I groused.

"Do you remember the girl or not?"

I mentally ran through my night, trying to come up with a face that stuck out. A blonde? What blonde? There'd been a really hot Korean waiter at MEJU, where we'd had dinner—the drive to Somerville from Grigor's mansion in Back Bay not even a thing with how much we were all craving something different. The whole week before we were holed up in an apartment building Grigor owned in Bratva while the dust settled on a slight misunderstanding with the Russians over a shipment of heroin. All things being equal, they'd taken several crates of cocaine off Grigor two weeks prior. It was just payback. Why they got all loud and serious when we retaliated was beyond me. It was, Grigor always said, the cost of doing business. You didn't win every time, and sweating the small stuff would only put you in an early grave. But even though it was mostly posturing, the best thing was to lie low and stay out of their way for at least five days. It was a general show of respect, acting like you were scared. They did it for us when the roles were reversed.

But hiding out meant we were stuck together with Grigor cooking because he liked to, and at home with his mother, he never got a chance. It always started out great, the stews he knew how to cook, like *pileći paprika*, which was a chicken one, the *gulaš*, or pork goulash, *slatki kupus*, which was basically a cabbage soup you could add meat to, and a variety of other fried stuff like *shufnoodles* with fried breaded crumbs, or *Karađorđeva šnicla*, translated "Karadjordje's steak," which was my favorite: a boneless, breaded pork steak. But still, no matter how good it was, God, by the end of the week, we were all dying for something, anything other than his cooking. So after we went home, showered and changed, and convened back at his mansion, I announced I was going for Korean, and suddenly everybody wanted that, would in fact die for that, if need be.

"Ceaton?"

I could not for the life of me place any blonde. "Man, I must have been really out of it, because I don't remember any girl."

"That's because you didn't seem interested, so after she checked your tonsils, she went home with Pravi."

And that made sense. Pravi was the smoothest guy I knew. He was all charm and heat with finely cut aristocratic features and between the rippling muscles, glorious tattoos, and thousand-dollar suits, women basically threw themselves at his feet.

"Everyone goes home with Pravi."

"I know," he groused.

"You need to learn to put on the accent like he does."

"I tried. It sounds stupid when I do it."

"Yeah."

"Don't agree with me, you asshole. You're supposed to be my friend."

"Oh yeah? If we're such good friends, how come you don't know that I would never be interested in a girl," I grumbled.

He cackled loudly. "You will never find a wife."

"You know I own a gun, right?"

More laughter from him before, "Fine, husband, whatever. Don't you want to settle down?"

"In our line of work? Really?"

"What?"

"C'mon, Luka. You know that death is always a very real possibility. You think that asking anyone to make that kind of commitment to me, to any of us, is a good idea?"

"You don't think guys in our line of business get married?"

I would not debate this with him.

"You have to think about your future."

"Uh-huh."

"*Jebi se*," he muttered under his breath. "Come have dinner. My mother wants you here."

The last time I'd had dinner with Luka and his mother, along with Marko and Pravi, halfway through dinner she'd turned in her chair and smiled at me.

"Mrs. Novak?"

"Ceaton," she sighed. "I want you to come to church with me on Thursday."

I glanced over at Marko, who gave me a quick shake of his head, and then at Pravi, whose grin could only be described as shit-eating. "I'm not really—" I coughed. "—a church guy, Mrs. Novak. In fact, I've never gone."

She clapped her hands happily. "Oh, this is wonderful news. Now I can be the one to take you and get you baptized. I'll be your sponsor."

I shot Luka a look that should have killed him. "Uh, you don't think that could be construed as hypocritical, considering what I do for a living?"

"No, dear," she assured me. "We all have a need for God's love in our lives, and you boys all—especially you," she stressed, pointing at Marko, "—need forgiveness."

"What have you been telling your mother about me?" Marko barked at Luka.

"Ma," Luka whined.

"But you, Ceaton," she cooed, taking the fork out of my hand so she could enfold it in both of hers, "are such a good boy, always worrying for the others, making sure they're safe. You need God in your life, and we have an LGBT night down at the rec center now."

I did a slow pan to Luka.

He wouldn't even look at me.

Pravi snickered as the doorbell rang.

"Oh, wonderful," she cheered, getting up to go to the front door.

"I'm gonna kill you," I assured Luka.

He put up his hands. "I didn't—oh."

And I saw Pravi stop eating mid-bite as he, too, turned to Luka.

Marko scoffed under his breath until the third girl, who'd apparently been hanging back, reached the doorway and then slipped inside.

"Not so funny now," Pravi rebuked.

"Come, come," Mrs. Novak gushed happily, guiding the women over to the table after draping their coats over the back of the couch.

There was Yuliana, Zuzana, and Hildur, and really, they all looked like they should have been in the Miss Universe pageant: simply stunning, statuesque women who really all belonged on the cover of a fashion magazine. I looked down at my plate and bit my lip so I wouldn't laugh my ass off right there.

"You have something to say?" Pravi growled at me through gritted teeth as Hildur was seated next to him.

"Mmmm-mmm," I muttered, not looking up, trying desperately not to smile.

"So Pravi," Mrs. Novak began, "Hildur is from Novi Sad."

Like he knew shit about Serbia. He was second generation American—only Grigor's family had been in the United States longer—and his Serbian was laced mostly with profanity because that was what he'd picked up. His mother, like Grigor's, spoke English at home. Both of Pravi's parents were Serbian, but that didn't mean he was in the market for a Serbian wife. Or any wife at all, for that matter, or even a commitment that lasted longer than a night. Neither of us was more than a one-and-done kind of guy.

"Oh," was all he could think of to say.

I put my face in my hand and covered my eyes, willing myself not to lose it.

"Marko, Yuliana is from Moscow."

That was it; I had to see my friend's face.

I looked up in time to see one of his thick, perfectly arched eyebrows lift before he said something to the young woman that made her gasp first, blush second, and then turn to look at me in absolute horror.

"He was raised in a barn," I assured her, smiling, giving her a gentle pat on the arm.

She put her hands under her chair and lifted it, scooching closer to me.

For his part, Marko rolled his eyes and went back to eating, just shoveling it in as Luka offered his "date," Zuzana, some of the roasted potatoes, keeping up a running discourse the entire time. It was hard to tell if he was into her or if it was a show for his mother. It didn't matter, though: fifteen minutes into the meal, all three women were leaning with their elbows on the table, staring at Pravi.

It was funny because, yes, he was sexy, and yes, there were the tattoos and the muscles, but you didn't notice all that at first. What you noticed was his laugh, and the way his eyes fired when he was talking about something that interested him, or how aristocratic his profile was. If he was walking, there was the strut to consider and the way his clothes hugged all the long, carved lines of him.

I was a fan.

I enjoyed looking at him myself, but I knew that underneath he was all player, through and through. Big, burly, brooding Marko never stood a chance, and Luka was handsome in a hot accountant or a school guidance counselor kind of way who seemed steady and solid. If you were looking for a husband, he was what you wanted. But if Pravi Radic was sitting at the table too… not so much.

They all left with the lothario on their way to some club.

I took Mrs. Novak's hand in mine. "Maybe bring over some less pretty ones next time. Some school teachers or nurses."

"*Da*," Marko agreed with me, still eating. "A nurse we could use."

"Nurse," Mrs. Novak said with a nod, clearly making a mental note, before smiling at me again. "So, Thursday?"

"I thought," I began uncomfortably, "that Catholics were not so good with homosexuality."

"Who told you such lies?" she wanted to know, clearly ready to squash whoever had dared to besmirch the good name of the Church.

She was the sweetest lady, always wanting us to take home food, always filling Tupperware and wrapping bread in foil and wanting to hug us all and touch our faces, comment on the length of our hair and remind us to drink less, exercise more, and above all, *get married.*

"Ceaton, honey," she said, smiling brightly. "Are we on for Thursday?"

Thank God we were busy that week, so I'd been able to miss the meeting at the rec center connected to St. Anne's downtown with a reasonable excuse.

"C," Luka snapped, bringing me back to the here and now. "Dinner? Yeah?"

"Tell her thank you, but I'm just gonna lie around and watch football. I'll see ya tomorrow."

"Your loss," he said curtly, and I knew why. No way in hell he wanted to be alone with his mother again. She grilled him when they were alone. The only reason I was getting crap from him about never getting married was because he heard the same song and dance from her.

"Bring me leftovers."

He grunted and hung up, which meant it was 50/50 on him bringing me food.

I was surprised when my phone rang again a moment later. I was not usually so popular. When I checked, the number said Private, but I answered anyway.

"Hello?"

"Ceaton" came my name on a sigh.

Jonas Bingham, my boss's lawyer. "Yeah," I said tightly, because why was I getting a call?

"What are you doing?"

"Nothing."

"Me too," he said, but no more.

I waited but all I got was silence. "And?" I asked to get things moving.

"And I'm here at home and was thinking you should come over."

It was not the first time he'd asked, but my answer would always be the same, even though lately, with the hours I was putting in, I rarely even had time to get out to a club and pick anybody up anymore. Since posting a profile on Grindr in my line of work was simply not possible, when Jonas called a month back—the first of many times since then—and offered up his ass, I actually thought about it for a full second and a half. But I knew how it would turn out because there was nothing about him that made me look twice to begin with, so it would be, as most of my encounters were, thoroughly forgettable. And because I didn't care, I simply said no. What was fortunate was I had a built-in excuse.

"I don't think so," I told him.

"And why not?"

"You know why not," I said flatly.

"No, I don't know. How about you enlighten me."

"How about you gimme a break and stop busting my balls."

"No, it's not like that."

"Then what is it like, Jonas, because you know Grigor's got rules."

"Oh, come on," he said, the sneer in his tone not lost on me.

I was quiet, letting him grapple with what he knew of my boss.

"Like Grigor Jankovic cares who either of us fucks."

That was true, or would have been if both of us didn't work for him. But as it was, Grigor *would* care simply because he made the rules and those rules were made to be followed. "What does he always say?" I asked Jonas.

"What?"

"Grigor," I prodded. "What does he say?"

"I have no idea what—"

"Don't shit where you eat."

"That's—"

"He says that all the time. When the new guys start, that's what he tells them."

"This is not the same thing at all."

"No?"

"Ceaton, you—"

"I think maybe you know him better'n me, then," I offered. "I think even though I've known him longer, that you've got the inside track with how his brain works."

"That's not what I'm saying."

"But for me," I went on, ignoring him, "I'm gonna need a few more assurances beyond your word, so you go ahead and get clarification from him, yeah?"

The silence that followed was not a surprise.

No fucking way did Jonas Graham have the balls to ask Grigor if he cared if the two of us were screwing. I smiled just imagining him leading into that conversation.

"I don't need to ask."

I snorted out a laugh that was not friendly. "That's because you know the answer already."

"You're wrong."

"I'm right, actually." And I was.

"How do you know?"

"I've seen it."

"Oh?" He sounded interested. "When was this?"

I was not going into it with him. He didn't need to know about Aram Babič and the dancer from a club Grigor used to manage before he moved up. I didn't even know the whole story—it happened before I joined his crew in Vegas—but from the pieces I'd been able to put together from things Marko had said… Grigor had lost his best friend.

Apparently the girl Aram loved had been his and Grigor's boss's favorite piece of ass. In the end, he killed Aram, and Grigor killed him. And yes, that led to Grigor taking over, but he would have liked to have had his childhood friend with him. After that, no one was allowed a dalliance in his household.

"Ceaton?"

"None of your business," I said gloomily.

"I think you're lying."

"About it being none of your business?"

"About there being a story to begin with."

"Really."

"Grigor knows you're gay, so why would it matter to him if you're sleeping with me? That makes no sense."

"It just would."

"Are you out or not?"

"I am," I answered, because I had never hidden who I was. No good could ever come of keeping secrets.

"Then I don't understand."

"The other guys don't get to bang the girls that dance in the clubs or any of the waitresses, so having you and I together would compromise Grigor's—"

"I'm not talking about us being anything other than a quick hookup."

And there it was. "Oh," I said quickly. "One-night stand. I misunderstood."

"Wait—"

"Problem solved, then."

"Ceaton—"

"You were just looking for a quick fuck."

"No, that's—"

So was I. Always. I was not looking for anything serious, and normally I was lucky to get first names. But this way, with Jonas, I could give him the brush-off and be the wounded party at the same time. It would ensure him actually leaving me alone, which was what I wanted. Grigor wouldn't put a bullet in me for banging his lawyer, but I didn't even want to have that talk with him about it. Ever. "It's no big deal. I'll see you around."

"I know you're not giving me the brush—"

I hung up because, really, what was the point? He'd shown his hand. I was nothing to him.

When my phone rang again—it was *insane* how popular I suddenly was—Private for a second time, I let it go to voice mail. At least it was done. There was comfort in that. Because no matter what Jonas thought, Grigor would not want to know I was screwing his lawyer. He'd be worried that, somehow, if for Jonas it came down to Grigor or me, Jonas would pick me if we were screwing. I knew better. Jonas would always side with the money.

The thing was, though, I didn't want to do anything to rock the boat with Grigor because lately he'd been looking at me oddly. It was more a feeling than anything else, but it felt like there was tension between us, and I had no idea why. It was like I was sitting in the middle of a giant chessboard and pieces were being moved into position without me knowing. Suddenly he wanted me to take someone new with me on a job instead of Luka or Pravi, he was keeping Marko with him constantly, and he was asking Doran to do things that were normally mine to handle. The issue with the Russians had been a bit of a mixed bag because, yes, we were stuck in close quarters for a week, but it was almost like we'd needed it—as though bonding had been necessary.

I was dozing again when the phone rang, *again*, what the fuck, and it was Marko.

"Hey," I greeted him.

"I need favor, yes?"

"Maybe. What is it?"

"Jonas Bingham, Grigor's lawyer. He needs to speak to you but does not have your number. I told him I could not give to him but I would have you call."

Shit.

"So you will do this?"

"I doubt he needs any—"

"Just call him so Grigor gives us no trouble."

"Okay," I agreed.

"Okay."

"Hey, wait."

He grunted.

"I didn't get a chance to talk to you alone at all last week."

"No."

"So what—you enjoying hanging with Grigor?"

"It matters little."

I cleared my throat. "You gettin' chummy with Doran?"

"Doran fears me; we cannot be friends because of this."

That made sense. "I asked Grigor to let you come back to work with me and Luka and Pravi, but he says he needs you with him."

"*Da*. Is you."

"Pardon?"

"He thinks—I do not know what he thinks. But others… they talk about you. They do not say Grigor, they say Ceaton."

"But that's what he wanted, remember? He wanted to be the public face of a legitimate company. He told us."

"*Da*, but being legitimate, there is no fear in that."

"Who cares?"

"He cares," he assured me. "People say, oh Grigor, he is worth so much, he has so much, but Mercer… do not cross Mercer, you will be dead by morning."

I scoffed. "No one says that."

"You are scary man, and you have scary men who are loyal to you. Why would Grigor not be threatened by such a man?"

"That's insane," I told him, annoyed, and I could hear it seeping into my voice. "So he's gonna do what, kill me based on what he thinks I want, who he thinks I am?"

"People are killed for less."

"Fuck."

"You asked."

"I gotta talk to him."

"Watch your back. I will watch Doran."

"Thanks."

"*Nye zaboyteya*."

"Oh, fuck you," I said, laughing. "That's not Serbian."

"I am Russian, you stupid prick," he informed me with a chuckle and hung up.

Instead of doing as I was asked and calling Jonas, I waited for the next Private number call and answered. "That was a shitty thing to do."

"You don't get to just cut me off."

"The hell I don't," I snapped. "Grigor is my boss, not you."

"Just calm down and—"

"Why the hell are you being so persistent? Get a life, Graham. Find some twink who gives a fuck that you're a rich douchebag lawyer."

Quick exhale of breath. "Look, I'm sorry, all right? That was a shitty thing to say earlier. I didn't mean it."

"Why does it matter?" I barked, more than annoyed now because I was worried about Grigor and this was a complication I didn't need.

"It matters, you matter."

"Since when?"

"Just—come over."

"Are you high on something?"

"No. Why would you think that?"

"Because you're being really strange," I grumbled. Then I wondered why he wanted me over there so badly. Was it a setup? "Is Grigor over there?"

"What?"

"Is Grigor at your place?"

"Have you lost—why would Grigor be at my place?"

I had to stop before I got good and paranoid. "Nothing. Never mind."

"Shit."

And that fast, I was back to him having some kind of breakdown. "What's going on with you?"

"I need to see you."

Need? "The hell for?"

He growled.

"Listen, I'm sure you know lots of guys you can call to come scratch your itch for you."

"I don't want just any guy."

But it was too late, and honestly, I didn't care. "Call somebody else. I'm beat," I said coolly—I could hear the ice starting to form in my tone.

"No, you're not."

"The hell I'm not!" I yelled, irritated, tired, with a stomach that was reacting to Grigor maybe or maybe not wanting me out of the way. It happened all the time, one day you were in tight with the boss, the next day you were dead in a ditch. I wasn't stupid; I knew it was a possibility. I'd just thought that Grigor and I were beyond any petty bullshit. But perhaps not.

"Just—"

"We had a fucked-up week!" I railed at Jonas because he was handy and I needed to vent my frustration on someone. "And last night we all stayed out way too late. It's lucky I'm even conscious right now!"

"Why?"

"Why what? Why am I tired?"

"Yeah."

"I just told you," I said, grimacing and feeling a sharp stab of pain. "Shit, owww."

"What's wrong?"

"My lip's split and you're making me—"

"I'm sorry?"

"I said my lip—"

"What happened?" he asked. I could hear the concern plain as day in his voice.

Well, shit. I couldn't be a total ass to him if he was going to keep being nice.

"You know," I croaked, my voice full of sand, the anger receding a fraction. "Perils of the job."

"You should quit and come work for me," he said hoarsely.

"What?"

"I said—" He coughed. "You should come work for me."

"Oh?"

"Yes. You could be our in-house investigator at the firm."

"Could I?"

"You could," he confirmed. "Easily."

"Easily," I echoed.

"Are you calling me a liar?"

"I said nothing of the kind."

There was a long silence.

"Just—Ceaton, you're made for better things than being muscle for Grigor Jankovic."

I cleared my throat. "I'm not qualified to do anything but what I currently do."

"We both know that's a lie."

"Is it?"

"Yes, it is," he said adamantly. "You're smart. You observe people and listen, and anytime Grigor needs to find anyone, he goes to you."

"You—"

"I've seen you, Ceaton. You find people all the time. That's how I know you'd make a fine private detective. All you need is your license, which should be simple enough to get."

"I—"

"Everybody likes you. Everybody wants to talk to you or do you a favor. It's all part of your charm."

"I carry a gun," I enlightened him. "That's why people talk to me."

"No, it's not. Stop acting like I haven't seen you do those things."

I grunted.

"I know you."

The hell he did. At that very moment there were three guys on the planet who knew anything about me at all, and he wasn't one of them.

If I'd been asked the night before, I would have counted Grigor as a friend too. But now, with just those few quick words with Marko... now... everything was different. Changed.

Suddenly I was back to where I was almost five years ago, standing on the side of the road, watching a car pull up in front of me. I was scared again, on shaky ground, unsure of whether to stay or go, run or stand my ground. This was fight or flight. If Grigor didn't trust me, what was there to win? His faith? Trust? Loyalty? Hadn't those all been proven years ago?

Not again. I couldn't go back to zero after I'd built so much.

My head was spinning, and Jonas Graham was not helping with the false platitudes designed to get him into my pants.

"Ceaton, I—"

"You don't know anything about me at all," I said, the warning in the sound of my voice, the sharpness of the delivery.

"I—"

"I do what I do for a reason, so don't start talking about us like we're friends."

"We're not friends," he agreed, and his tone was icy. "But I know more about you than you think I do, and I also know that you're smarter than you give yourself credit for."

"When I hang up this time, don't call Marko again, yeah?"

"Just—you have other options," he insisted. "Legitimate offers, legal offers. You need to use your brain for once and think past today."

He had a point. Falling asleep in your suit because you were drunk and bleeding did not speak to using one's brain. I needed to slow down, stop drinking so much, and realize I wasn't going to die at thirty because I was already a year past that. I needed to figure out a real plan for my life because being muscle for Grigor was neither a good one, nor, it seemed, one with much of a future.

"Are you listening to me?"

No.

"Ceaton?"

"Sorry, what?"

"I said you could do something else."

"Like what?"

"As I said, I could find a place for you at the firm."

"Oh yeah? Does it involve fucking you?"

"I would not be opposed to that."

"Give it a rest."

"You're driving me crazy."

"Yeah, well, you'll get over it," I said and hung up on him. I was surprised that he called right back. *Again.* "The hell's the matter with you?!" I roared, sitting up, *so* ready to hurl my phone across the room. "Are you deaf?"

"I want to see you!"

"There are a hundred guys that'll give you what you need!" I half yelled. "And they'd all love to have you fuck 'em. What's with you being all persistent and shit?"

Silence.

"You don't need me to get laid."

"You're very crude."

I sighed. "You so haven't heard crude, if you think that was it."

"Ceaton—"

"And I think that's most of what you like about me: my crudeness."

"Not at all. You're far more appealing than you think."

I chuckled as I rolled sideways and realized I was lying on my gun. Not good to sleep on your gun. Not good for a Sig Sauer P226, not good for the body. The safety was on, of course, so there was no worry about it going off, but still…. How tired did I have to be to just drop into bed? There were blood smears on my sheets too.

"Shit," I grumbled.

"What's wrong?"

"I've got blood on my Egyptian cotton sheets," I muttered. "I see bleach in my future."

"You're worried about your sheets?"

"They're nice sheets," I groused.

"Ceaton—"

"Look, why don't you just call any of the other—"

"They are not—they cannot—"

"What?"

"Only you… ever… said…. You promised to…. Ceaton."

Oh. His reasoning finally sank through my brain. We'd had one talk that explained his doggedness, and now I remembered the particulars. "You need me because the other boys only bottom."

I heard his deep exhale of breath.

"And that's not what you're craving right now."

He hung up then. I understood. It was a little too much honesty, a little too much confession. It was one thing to call and arrange to fuck. It was another to have to explain what you needed.

When my phone beeped with the ringtone set for Grigor, I took a breath before I answered, trying to let all the irritation seep out of my voice before I picked up. "Hey," I greeted Grigor as I answered.

"Where are you?"

"At home, why?"

"I need you to come here."

Which meant he couldn't say whatever it was on the phone. "Do I have time to shower?"

"Shower and pack a bag."

I grimaced, thankful he couldn't see me. Would a break be so out of the question? "For how long?"

"I hope only three days."

Christ.

The last time I got directions like that, I ended up in Reno getting rid of seven bodies for him. I hoped it was something less strenuous. Lye was a messy business, and cleaning up well was exhausting. I made a noise without meaning to.

"Did you just whine?"

And the snicker in his tone, the fondness, almost took my breath away. Because if he could sound like this on the phone, familiar, jovial, teasing—then we had to be okay and I was freaking out for no good reason. "I… what? No."

He chuckled. "You don't have to leave the state."

I perked up a bit. "Oh no?"

"No. I just need you to keep track of something for me."

This was new. "What kinda something?"

"I'll tell you when you arrive."

"Could you be more cryptic?"

"I could, yes. I think so." Grigor really did not do well with sarcasm, but still, when he sighed—and I heard it… I could breathe again.

"I'm jumping in the shower."

"Good. Hurry."

I tried not to worry all over again when he hung up.

CHAPTER FOUR

WHEN I got to the mansion in Back Bay, once I went through the enormous wrought-iron front gate and rolled up on the half-circle drive, I realized I was looking at more than thirty cars. Something bad was happening, so I parked my 1971 Land Rover—completely out of place with the sleek sports cars and high-end SUVs—and darted toward the front steps. I got a head tip from each of the four men guarding the door, and slipped inside. I listened for his voice, heard yelling, and walked not toward his office, but the great room.

Grigor was on the phone, pacing in front of a lit fireplace and working himself up, yelling in Serbian, jaw clenched, neck muscles corded, and free hand flailing, then fingers raking through the thick, coarse black hair that fell to his shoulders.

"What's going on?" I asked the other six men in the room.

Reagan Corbett, his accountant, left the bar where he was drinking and crossed the room to me. "We just found out that the shipment we've been waiting on from Budapest was picked up by Ivan Aristov's men."

The Russian mob, the Irish mob, a Columbian cartel, a Mexican cartel—who took it hardly mattered. Gone was gone, and now people who were waiting on product would have to go somewhere else to get it unless a suitable solution was found.

"But more importantly," Seth Jaffe, Corbett's right-hand man, began from where he sat on the couch, with a tumbler of scotch, "the cops found Pavle, Goran, and Sava all shot in the back of the head at Sava's club in Dorchester this morning."

What I heard was "moore" and then "Dorchestah this moningh." Jaffe had the accent, the Boston one you heard so much about. Not being a native—having come late to the party—I'd never picked it up.

It was strange news. On one hand they were guys I knew, and though not particularly nice ones—especially Sava, whose homicidal temper was legendary—it was still surreal that they were gone. On the other hand, men in Grigor's business did not, as a rule, live to be old men, so it was not surprising that they were gone, either. We'd lost many over the years. Only me and the four others who came from Vegas together remained. I credited it to us watching out for one another. Even Luka's mother—who moved here, just like Grigor's, to be near him—kept an eye on the rest of us.

"What about their families?" I asked automatically.

"We're making sure they're taken care of," Seth assured me. "Grigor had me setting up trust funds right after we got the news."

I nodded. "That's good."

He shrugged. "Least we could do, yeah?"

It was.

"C." Turning, I found myself the focus of Grigor's attention. He gestured for me to approach him, and I crossed the room at his invitation. When I was close enough, he put a hand on my shoulder. "Aca says you hung up on him when he called you today."

I waited because I knew better than to worry, at least about that. If Grigor was going to turn on me, it would not be over his worthless cousin who annoyed all of us. His question was about Aca, not me. "I did."

"Tell me," he prodded, already looking pained, long-suffering, wincing over what I was going to say.

"If he maybe didn't want to talk about going on a run for you while he was on the phone with me… that might be good, huh?"

He groaned as Pravi walked in and headed over to us.

"What's wrong?" he asked Grigor, even as he glanced at me and then back to our boss.

"Does Aca talk business with you on the phone too?"

"He tries," Pravi confirmed. "I hang up."

"*Govno*," Grigor said under his breath.

It meant "shit." I smiled because it was one of the first words I learned. "Small wonder I can't converse in polite society in Serbian," I teased Pravi.

He nodded because the point could not be argued.

Grigor punched a button on his cell's display and put the phone to his ear. Aca must have answered because he snarled "*Tvoj ćale bolje da je izdrkao nego što je tebe napravio,*" after a moment and then yelled for several more minutes.

When I looked at Pravi again, he shook his head as he pressed his lips together. Apparently whatever was being said was *really* not good.

"He's just a kid," I said, trying to make an excuse for Aca, my words directed at Pravi.

"He's a menace," Grigor retorted, having stopped yelling at his cousin for a second. "And you know that."

I did, but I also knew he could learn if given the chance.

Grigor got off his phone and tossed it onto the couch before he turned to Pravi. "Go pick him up."

Pravi gave me a head tip before he turned to leave. Grigor faced me next.

"I have a favor to ask you."

Since when did he ask? He didn't ask; he told. "Course," I said, even though it was unneeded.

He cleared his throat. "I need you to go out to Nahant and look after Judge Ammon Hardin's son."

Grigor had so many judges on his payroll, it was hard to keep track. "Which one is Hardin?"

"He's the one running for district attorney next year."

"The ten-grand-a-month one?"

"Yes."

"And?"

"And I need you to go out to Nahant."

"Which is where?"

"Just outside Boston."

"Okay." I was confused because what he was saying made no sense. "I seem to remember that the son lived in New York," I said to Grigor. "Didn't me and Luka have to go up there to pay off some woman who took pictures of him at a party snorting cocaine and fucking some guy?"

"Yes."

"And Hardin's daughter, she's the one who went to rehab in Aspen."

He nodded.

"So what kid lives here?"

"The illegitimate one."

"Who?"

He cleared his throat. "Brinley Todd, Judge Hardin's youngest son, is doing research at the Northeastern University Marine Science Center, which is there in Nahant."

"Rewind, I just woke up."

He waved a dismissive hand. "You know how these things go."

"Normally, yeah, but since when does a mistress of a powerful man get to have a kid?"

"Apparently the judge's family, the Hardins, and his wife's family, the Kellogs, wheeled and dealed and got their children together when he was attending Harvard and she was at Radcliffe."

Why did he know all this, and was I supposed to care? "Since when are you and the judge so cozy?"

His scoff was loud.

"What? Do you golf together now?"

He ignored the comment. "Hardin is helping me make several of the businesses legitimate. You know that."

I did. "What does any of this have to do with his bastard?"

"He doesn't think of him like that."

"I care why?"

"He loved Brinley's mother."

Not enough to get a divorce. "Sure he did."

"You don't have a romantic bone in your body."

Sacrifice was romantic. Taking a hit to the wallet and reputation for someone you loved… that spoke volumes to me. Living in a loveless marriage for prestige and money was not any romantic ideal I'd ever heard of.

"Hardin told me that he met Brinley's mother at a fundraiser. She was there waitressing, and he was blindsided by her humor and warmth."

Grigor didn't talk like that; he was repeating something the judge had told him.

"He lied to her, took off his wedding ring, told her they would be together."

"When did she find out the truth?"

"Her parents were in town, and it turned out that they had friends in common with Hardin and his wife. So when everyone met up to attend the ballet, they crossed paths, and Erin Sullivan learned the truth about Ammon Hardin."

"That's awful."

"Erin was, Hardin said, the soul of discretion and never once let on that she had ever met him. She made sure to sit by his wife, however, and learn everything about where they lived, his kids, and how long they'd been married.

"When he went to see Erin later that night, she had all his things that he'd ever left at her place boxed up and ready to go."

"And when did she tell him about Brinley?"

"She didn't. He found out from his wife when she bumped into Erin on the street and found out Erin was pregnant."

I was impressed with Erin for wanting nothing to do with a cheating piece of crap like Hardin. "Did he call her right away?"

"He didn't. He didn't want anything to do with her or her son."

"Even though he knew the kid was his?"

"She's the one who ended things."

I laughed. "I know you. Some woman gets knocked up with your kid, you'll support them both the rest of their lives."

He grimaced but gave me a reluctant nod.

"So what happened with the judge?"

"He kept tabs on them and finally offered Erin some help."

"Which she said no to."

"All except one thing."

I knew what it was without him telling me. "College money."

"Yes. The only thing Erin would allow him to do for either of them over the years was put money in an account so that Brinley would have funds at his disposal for when he was ready to get his degree."

"Smart lady."

"Agreed."

There had to be more. "And?"

"And now he needs help."

"Hardin or the son?"

"Hardin."

"So he reached out to you?"

"Yes."

"For what reason?"

"Apparently Hardin has received threats about our business dealings that he has, of course, been hesitant to report to the authorities."

I would expect so. Judge Hardin had been on the take for so long that he and many of the other judges and assistant district attorneys he knew would all be compromised if any link between him and Grigor was ever established. Having the FBI digging around in his and Grigor's relationship would be a nightmare.

"So now what?"

"Hardin was told that if he didn't play ball—"

"With who?" I interrupted. "Who's leaning on him?"

"I think Djordjevic and McNamara, but I'm not sure. I'm looking into it."

Anton Djordjevic had come from Chicago a year ago and, being Serbian as well, made contact with Grigor as soon as he hit town. But it became quickly apparent that he was much more interested in taking over Grigor's operation than in being friends. He also was flashy and his gang was violent, with no respect at all for how things were done. He'd promptly gotten in bed with the Irish and Russian mob, making things awkward with Grigor, who already had deals in place with the Colombians and the Italians. Because Grigor and Djordjevic were, supposedly, on the same side, it made for tense meetings whenever they crossed paths. Sooner or later, I knew there would be a reckoning.

"So they're trying to recruit your people by threatening their families?"

"They tried blackmailing a couple of others, but Marko and Pravi took care of that and sent a message at the same time."

I didn't want to know. "But for Hardin, they threatened his son."

"Not only his life, but sharing the secret of his parentage."

"You can't do anything about that."

"No one can. Erin never put anyone down as the father on the birth certificate, so there's nothing concrete that links them."

"Then what?"

"Someone finally looked into who the college fund went to."

"Following the money is always smart."

"Yes."

"So the trail led straight to the illegitimate son."

"It did."

"But money alone doesn't prove anything."

"No, but it looks bad. Because if Hardin isn't related to Brinley, then he's an older man giving a younger guy money, and that begs the question… for what?"

"Hardin is worried about what? Looking like a sugar daddy?"

"No. Hardin isn't worried about his secret getting out at all. What he's worried about is his son's safety."

"Okay. Has anything happened so far?"

"This morning they called and told Hardin that they already had Brinley, but he called and confirmed that Brinley was at his home in Nahant and that nothing was wrong at the moment."

"So Hardin and his kid are close now?"

"Not close, but apparently his mother told him years ago who his father is, and they've maintained a polite relationship ever since."

"What does that even mean?"

"It means that if they talk on the phone, they're nice to each other."

"Ah."

"Hardin said that Brinley was surprised to hear from him, but they spoke for several minutes, and during that conversation he told his son that he was having issues with a criminal element and that Brinley, as well as his other children, might be in danger."

"And Brinley bought that?"

"His father's a judge. Is it so farfetched that he would be threatened?"

I shrugged.

"After Hardin got off the phone with Brinley, that's when he called me."

"So he asked you to provide protection for his son."

"Yes."

I sighed loudly because, seriously? This was what I was good for?

"What?"

"Shouldn't I be the one going to talk to Djordjevic?"

He shook his head. "I can't do anything to Anton directly. I'd have trouble from Belgrade and McNamara—he's a favorite Irish son."

"That doesn't mean that everyone under them is off-limits."

"I agree," he snapped, which wasn't like him. "Do you think I don't know?"

I scowled at him. "What's with you?"

He shook his head. "I've let you handle these kinds of matters for too long."

"What's that supposed to mean?"

He met my gaze. "I have to strike back at Aristov today for Pavel, Goran, and Sava."

"So you know he did that?"

Quick nod. "Doran found out already."

"And you want to handle that yourself instead of letting me take care of it?"

"I think I have to."

"Why's that?"

"I can't maintain control if I distance myself any further than I already have," he said flatly. "Everyone says to me, 'Oh, Ceaton's going to kill them.'"

I stood there trying to read his face.

"So you're the hand of God, and I'm what?" Grigor posed.

"I think that's how it's supposed to be."

He shook his head. "No. *I* am God, not you."

Nothing I said would be good here.

The smile he forced did nothing to make me feel any better. "I'll deal with Aristov, and then I'll go talk to Djordjevic and McNamara."

"And I'll do what? Go out and babysit this kid?"

His face tightened. "This is my business, right?"

"No, I know that, but seriously, you could have anyone sit on this guy."

He cleared his throat and took a step closer to me. "This is—I trust you. Only you."

"Grigor—"

"The judge knows things about me, I know things about him, and neither one of us wants anyone else in the loop."

Why it needed to be me was starting to make more sense.

"The judge needs to see that I'm taking this situation very seriously. He needs to see that my best man is there with his son."

My gaze met his.

"Does it make sense now?"

It did, yes, and I was feeling better as well because it was starting to sound like the trust I'd been worried was waning was, in fact, still very much in place.

"After I got off the phone with Hardin, I called his son."

"Why?"

"I wanted to remind him who I was."

"You know Hardin's son?"

"Of course. Why wouldn't I?"

After I thought about it a moment, it made perfect sense. If someone had a weakness, Grigor made a point of finding out who or what that was. In Hardin's case, his weakness was his illegitimate son.

"How long have you known his son?"

"Only since the summer. That's when I first learned who he was."

"I see. And what did you talk about with the judge's son?"

"I explained that his father had asked me to provide him with some protection and that I would be sending a few men over to do just that."

"Wait. I thought you wanted me to—"

"I needed to see what he said."

More testing. "I see."

"Brinley told me in no uncertain terms that if he was going to have a bodyguard, that there had better be only one."

"So this kid, he thinks his father has hired protection for him."

"Yes."

"But really, I don't get why Hardin wouldn't just do that. Some of those private security guys are ex-Special Forces and Secret Service and shit like that."

"True. But this is a personal matter. Hardin doesn't want to have to explain to a company why this particular man needs protection."

"The whole bastard thing. Okay, I get it."

"And if Hardin came clean to the Feds, they would want to know about the threats and why they're being made. Asking me keeps things quiet."

True. "And his son—"

"Brinley."

"Brinley—he's just going to let me into his house?"

"Yes."

I shrugged. "I guess since he's willing to go along with whatever you and Hardin say, then there's—"

"He's not."

"He's not what?"

"He thinks his father is being ridiculous, and he told me that he doesn't want to have anything to do with anyone protecting him."

"But?"

"But he came to the Fourth of July party I had here at the mansion, and he saw you," Grigor said, giving me a trace of a smile.

"Me?" I jolted, confused and immediately tense. I didn't like to be noticed, never liked being seen, preferring to fade into the background. But now Grigor was telling me that I had most certainly been picked out of the crowd. "Are you sure?"

His eyes widened. "Am I sure what? That he saw you?"

"Yeah."

"Yes, Ceaton, he described you perfectly."

That made no sense.

Grigor squinted at me. "Why is this such a surprise?"

"He saw me?"

Grigor crossed his arms. "You think, what, that you're so forgettable?"

"Well, yeah."

He shook his head. "He walked into the pool."

"Who did?"

"Brinley."

"Why?"

"Because he was watching you."

I waited a moment. "Are you screwing with me?"

"No, I'm not screwing with you!" he replied irritably. "For fuck's sake, Ceaton, you're not a leper or something."

"So what now?"

"Don't sound so pained."

I couldn't help it. A lot of things were going through my head at the same time. Did Grigor actually need me to watch the judge's son? Was I, in fact, the one he trusted or had this all been initiated by this Brinley? And if that was the case, then Marko was right and I was still squarely in Grigor's crosshairs. I wanted to go back to yesterday, when everything made perfect sense and I knew where I stood, but I couldn't get my mind there. I couldn't relax and just have faith in Grigor's words instead of what Marko had filled my head with. The lack of caffeine wasn't helping any either. Trying to sort out truth from a possible lie was far too hard on only one cup of coffee.

"Hey," Grigor snapped.

"Sorry," I replied absently.

His face softened as he smiled, and I wasn't crazy about that either. Since when did he try to placate me when he was giving me an order?

"Listen, you didn't see the havoc you caused with him because you had to leave with Luka and Pravi to take care of the break-in at Strobe."

And maybe I was being paranoid—I probably was. We'd been together a long time now, and so it could be argued that our relationship would change, and could, at any moment. Did other people simply notice when they grew in importance in other people's lives? I'd always had trouble reading affection in others. Maybe Grigor and I were closer than I thought.

"It was like Brinley was struck by lightning when he saw you."

Or maybe I was being lulled into a false sense of security right before he shot me in the back of the head, just like he had his old boss. Grigor did have a reputation for dropping people when they least expected it.

"Are you listening to me?" He snarled, and I heard it then, the velvet he was going for that stretched thin across his prickling, barbed anger.

"Yes," I answered flatly.

He took a breath. "As I was saying, you didn't see the trouble you caused."

"*I* caused? I think I was here for, like, ten minutes that day."

"It was enough."

"For *what*?"

"For him to see you."

He really wanted me to hear him on this Brinley thing. It was important for me to get that it was Brinley who wanted me there and not Grigor. He wanted it made clear that it was the kid's idea completely. "Okay," I replied, playing along. Whatever this was, I'd know soon.

The noise he made was full of exasperation. "We were all worried that Brinley had hit his head, but it turned out, no, he just walked right into the deep end."

"And this has what to do with me?"

"He was looking at you, Ceaton, and couldn't do anything else."

What was I supposed to say? I couldn't very well tell him that I was sitting on the fence between thinking he was trying to kill me and thinking that some kid had me mixed up with someone else.

I was having the weirdest day already.

"So," Grigor huffed—exasperated, I could tell. He was scowling and breathing through his nose. "You will go now and look in on Hardin's son and make certain he lets you stay and protect him."

I wasn't done prodding. "Why don't you just send Pravi or Marko?"

"Because, as I said, you're the only one he agreed to see."

"But really," I said, my voice dropping, smirking at him. "Since when does anyone get a say in what you decide to do, even if he is a judge's son?"

"Since things aren't going as well as I'd like."

And there it was, another wrinkle. Because a distracted Grigor could account for any coldness and even for Marko thinking that our boss was up to something sinister.

Motherfuckinghell.

"Will you do this for me?"

I had no choice. Grigor was my boss, and if I wanted to keep my job, and more importantly, my life… I'd do what he said.

"Ceaton?"

"Of course."

"Good," he said as he gave my shoulder a pat. "Let me give you the address."

CHAPTER FIVE

NAHANT WAS a small island off the coast south of Salem, actually two islands connected together and to the mainland by a causeway built during the Great Depression as one of FDR's New Deal work programs. I'd lived in Boston for years and never been there, as close as it was—only about fifteen miles or so from Back Bay. But Grigor's business kept me busy, and since there was no call for me or any of the other guys to be out in Nahant, I'd never made the short trip a priority.

It was overcast as I made the drive: 1A North past Logan Airport, through Revere to Lynn. Before I got on the Nahant Causeway, I stopped for a late lunch and had a plate of Clams Casino and a Caesar salad, and washed it down with a vodka martini because I could and God knew when I'd have alcohol again. I had no clue what Brinley had at his house. The waitress explained several movies had been made in Lynn, and several even included the restaurant. It was nice to chat, and I asked some questions about Nahant.

"Wait'll you see the sunsets out there," she offered cheerfully. "It's gorgeous."

I smiled at her in return.

"How about another drink?"

It would have been fine, two drinks with how big I was, body weight to liquor ratio… but in good conscience I couldn't, and had ice tea to finish up.

"You visiting a friend in Nahant?"

I explained about my buddy being a grad student at Northeastern and that he was doing some kind of serious grant research at the marine science station.

"He sounds really smart."

Yes, he did.

Once I was done, I got on the causeway, and ten minutes later I was driving through a tiny town that, as far as I could tell, had no stoplights. It was odd going from Boston to this, and I wondered how quickly being in so small a place would drive me nuts. I was a nightlife guy; I liked fast, and if I was honest with myself, I knew why. If everything was a blur, I didn't have to think or feel or anything, and I liked that just fine. If I concentrated on what I didn't have—home, family, somebody permanent—it hurt. As long as I was moving at the speed of sound, nothing could get to me.

The GPS chirped as I drove down Nahant Road, passing the police station, town hall, and library when, after a couple of quick turns, I was on Willow Road being directed to the address of a sweet little cottage with three men on its porch.

After parking my ancient Land Rover in the driveway, I got out, turned, and was struck by the look on the face of the shortest of the three, the one who had moved to the railing to get a better look at me. The smile he directed my way was blinding, and between that and how warm his eyes were, I froze.

He exhaled, and I saw my name form on his lips even though from where I was, I couldn't hear him.

What the hell was this now?

Lifting my hand in greeting, I started forward again, and he came down the three steps onto the cobblestone path that led toward the gate. We met each other halfway.

"Hi," he sighed when he reached me, stepping in close and tilting his head back so he could see my face. Since he was maybe five eight, five nine, and I was six two, there was quite the height difference to make up.

I tried to step back so he wouldn't get a crick in his neck, but he reached out and lightly fisted his hand in my heavy gray wool sweater, the part over my chest that wasn't covered by my peacoat, not tight, but enough to stop me from moving.

"Hey," I said softly, matching his tone, not offering him my hand for some reason, feeling like that would be weird.

"Thank you for coming," he said, his gaze all over me like he was taking inventory. "I really appreciate it, but I've changed my mind."

"I'm sorry?" I asked, glancing at the two guys who joined us, both in jeans and heavy jackets and smiling at me as well. Brinley himself was in tan-colored corduroys and a heavy beige wool sweater coat with a shawl collar and oversized buttons that made him look even younger than he probably was.

He swallowed quickly, dropped his hand, and then forced a smile that didn't reach his eyes. "I tried to call my father to tell him not to have you come after all, but I couldn't reach him."

I searched his face because that made no sense. Why would his father screen his calls when he was worried enough about him to call Grigor? "Really," I said easily, glancing at the men flanking him. "Who're you guys?"

The one on the right cleared his throat and offered me his hand. "I'm Chris Eames, and this is Tate Cayson. We're Todd's buddies from school."

I nodded, taking in that lie. Todd, huh? Friends, my ass. They didn't even know Todd was his last name, not his first. "What're you doin' here?"

"Oh," Chris said jovially, "we're renting the little cottage Todd has in the back of his place, right off the garden."

"Is that right," I said to Brinley, who was looking up at me with his big, beautiful dark brown eyes utterly teeming with fear and uncertainty as a slight tremble rolled through his compact frame.

"Yes," he said quickly, shivering a little in the wind. It was not surprising he was cold. The wind was blowing icy and brisk off the water and playing havoc with the thick black mane of his that fell to surprisingly wide shoulders. Even though he was shorter than me, with fragile, delicate features, he was built strong with tight, lean muscles. He was more gymnast than lithe dancer. "It'll be so nice to have roommates."

Could his voice be any hollower? "Oh yeah?"

"Absolutely."

I looked away from him to Chris and Tate. "So are you guys all out at the marine science center together?"

"Yeah," Chris said quickly.

"You're doing research too?"

"Exactly," Tate chimed in.

"You study great white sharks, like Todd?" I asked, pulling that out of my ass, sounding like it was the coolest thing I'd ever heard.

"We sure do."

I knew little kids who lied better than these two. "That's great," I said, turning back to Brinley. "Must be nice to have guys you go to school with around, huh?"

He nodded, forcing another smile before he closed his eyes for a moment, untangling some stray strands of hair from thick lashes that looked like delicate glossy black feathers on his pale cheek. Pretty did not do the man justice; he was simply stunning. I had no idea how I'd missed him at any party we might have ever attended at the same time.

"We should go in," Chris said, slipping a hand over Brinley's shoulder. "It feels like it's getting colder by the second out here."

Brinley opened his mouth to say something to me.

"Let me at least get the food out of the car that Grigor sent with me." I yawned but remained focused on Brinley. "You know how much he likes to cook, and there's no fucking way I'm driving all the way home with it in my car. It smells bad enough now!"

If Brinley thought my words were odd, he didn't say anything, just nodded like that was all perfectly normal.

"It's hot," I explained. "Can you run inside and get some pot holders, and I'll have your buddies give me a hand with pies and bread he sent."

Brinley nodded and bolted toward the house. Both men moved to follow.

"Hel-*lo*," I snapped, which stopped them. "I wanna get outta here. This is not my idea of a good time, so can you fuckin' help?"

It made sense, and I'd played right into their hands. More than anything they wanted me gone, so they turned to do whatever I needed done.

"Food's in the back," I explained before returning at a jog to my Range Rover. "You guys are gonna have to make a few trips. Grigor never does anything small," I called over to them, making sure to put laughter into my voice as I opened the passenger-side door and pretended to get something out of the floorboard while I dug into the side pocket of my duffel for the Osprey silencer that fit the Sig I now had in my other hand.

"He really doesn't need any supplies," Chris insisted. "Just take it with you; we really have to go in before we all turn into popsicles."

"Okay," I agreed, then extended my arm and took aim.

"Shit!" Tate yelled before I shot him in the chest. Chris I got in the back of the head because he pivoted to run.

I quickly shoved my Sig back into the shoulder holster inside my coat as I saw Brinley appear at the door, ready to come out.

"Sorry," he said, raising his voice so it would reach me across the yard. "I couldn't find where I put—"

"It's okay," I said, stopping him before he stepped one foot out on the porch.

"Did somebody yell?"

I shook my head. "Nope."

"Are you guys all right out there?"

"Absolutely," I called back.

"Do you need any—"

"Could you make some tea?"

"Tea?" he asked, as though that was a completely foreign request on a cold day.

"Yeah."

"I have coffee. I don't know if I have any tea."

"Could you look?"

He squinted. "Yeah, I—what about the other—"

"Please."

His smile really was beautiful, and I saw him sigh more than heard it. There was no doubt about it, he wanted to make me happy, and if tea would do it, by God he'd look. "I'll find some, don't worry."

"Not worried," I assured him.

I got a last longing look before he closed the door behind him, disappearing back into the house.

It was a sleepy little street on a chilly Sunday, no one else was there, and not a soul had seen me gun down two men in cold blood, but I still moved fast because I didn't want to push my luck.

Returning to the Range Rover, I opened the back and grabbed the mattress cover I kept rolled up and ready to go. Something I'd learned years ago: the handy-dandy protective fitted covers that went over beds were much easier to carry around than heavy wool blankets and much more manageable than tarps. Plus, a twin-size mattress cover was just the right size, draped over my shoulder, to carry a man. They were made to keep a bed pristine, protected from all kinds of things, and they worked liked a charm to keep blood off clothes. Marko always said that a rain poncho would do the same thing, but if you had to stash someone in the back of your car, a poncho couldn't cover the entire area, whereas the mattress pad could be stretched out and then tucked around the body. We went back and forth on it, but I'd never been disappointed with my choice. So once I had it draped over me, I walked over to Chris, hoisted him up onto my shoulder in a fireman's carry, and pulled my phone out with my free hand and punched the display with my thumb.

"Ceaton?"

"Boss," I greeted him as I started around the side of the small house. "Brinley wants to play cards, so will you send Marko and Pravi out here so we can have a game?"

He was quiet for a moment. "So soon?"

"Yeah." I clipped the word because, of course, we weren't talking about poker. But we had to speak in code when every federal agency around was listening in on all our conversations. We'd worked this out years ago.

"I'll send them now. Do you need them to bring anything?"

"Just the regular stuff," I sighed, because plastic wrap, garbage bags, lye, and shovels would be in the van when they showed up. "And maybe some beer."

"No worries. I'm glad you're there to play cards with him."

"Yeah, me too," I assured him, ending the call and continuing around the now-hibernating rose garden to a tool shed.

It was a good place to store corpses, so I shoved Chris in, sprinted back, and then stacked Tate on top of his buddy, arranged them to make the most of the space, tight together, next to the weed whacker and some cans of paint before covering them both with the now blood-splotched mattress cover. Once I was done, I walked back to the house, taking a detour to grab my duffel out of the backseat and lock up my car.

I had to wait a couple of minutes after knocking on the door before Brinley opened it, smiling sheepishly, biting his bottom lip.

"I'm still looking for the tea."

"Oh, that's okay. I'm more of a coffee drinker anyway. I'm just trying to be better about the caffeine, so I thought—maybe he's got some tea."

"Caffeine is actually not bad for you," Brinley apprised me as he stepped aside to let me inside. He glanced over my shoulder, checking for the others before stepping out onto the porch and looking around the yard. "Where did they go?"

It was odd, he was right. The front lawn was small, ending at the quaint little white picket fence and the gate. On the left side of the house was the attached garage, on the right he had the path that led around back to the shed—where I'd just been—and the mother-in-law cottage the guys had lied about renting. The backyard was small too, but there was still enough space between the house and the cottage to grant some semblance of privacy. The thing was, though, all of it sat on maybe a quarter of an acre of land, and so from where he was standing now, he should have been able to see Chris and Tate.

"Did they go out back?"

"Come inside," I directed.

He moved quickly, closing the door behind him before stepping in front of me to stare into my eyes.

"So I'm the bodyguard, right?"

"I'm sorry?"

"I'm the bodyguard," I reiterated.

"No, I understand that, but what does that have to do with the food?"

"What food?" I asked, dropping my duffel on the wingback chair beside the couch before rounding on him.

"The food in the car."

Was he kidding? "There's no food. Why would there be food?"

He gave me an enigmatic smile, unsure but amused at the same time. "I don't know. You're the one who said there was."

"Why would Grigor make you food? He doesn't even know you."

"Which is why it was odd when you said it, but I didn't want to be rude," he clarified. "And then I thought, home cooking sounds kind of good, so I was hoping there was food, but now you're saying there's really not any."

"No."

"Oh, that's too bad," he said, deflating.

He was so odd. "Okay, now listen—"

His face brightened. "Did they leave?"

"What?"

"The agents," he prodded. "Did they go?"

Agents? "Sorta."

"How do people sort of leave?"

"When they don't actually but you'll never see them again."

He thought about that, and I could tell the second he came to the correct conclusion.

His eyes widened, his mouth dropped open into an O of total shock and disbelief, and his lovely sort of creamy complexion, peach mixed with just a flush of gold, leached to ash. When his breath caught, I knew we were in trouble.

"Okay," I said along with the first "eep" that came out of him followed instantly by a wheeze. "Hold on."

Scooping him up, one arm under his knees, the other supporting his back, I got him to the overstuffed couch and deposited him on it. I rushed to the kitchen, ransacked the cabinets, and found some Ziploc quart-size bags—because really, who had brown paper anymore—and returned to him, folding the opening up so he could breathe shallowly into the bag.

I watched as several minutes went by and he gave me the side-eye, making sure I stayed put. I was pleased that he didn't look scared, that I wasn't the one causing him to hyperventilate, but still.

He finally lifted his head and really looked at me.

"You all right?"

"So they're dead."

"Yes."

"Did you put them in your car?"

"No, I put them in your toolshed."

He absorbed that. "They can't stay there; the smell would alert the neighbors."

His calm was freaking me out just a little. "I have some of my associates coming to pick them up."

"People you trust?"

"Absolutely, yes."

"And you would do the same for them? Dispose of dead bodies?"

I nodded.

He was thinking again, weighing things out in his head, I could tell. "Are you gonna faint?"

Instant scowl.

"It's a reasonable question. Things looked a little dicey there for a second."

"I was just surprised. You were very casual with your delivery."

I had been. "I'm used to it."

"Well, you should consider your audience."

It shouldn't have been funny, listening to him scold me, but it was and I liked it, and liked him. "Why aren't you scared?"

"Of what?"

"How about me, for starters?"

He considered my words, looking at me. "You're here to protect me, aren't you?"

I was. "I am."

"Well, then," he said quietly, the laugh lines in the corner of his eyes crinkling.

Brinley was disarmingly easy to be around. I stood up to try to create some distance.

"Where are you going?"

I walked to the window and looked out at the yard. Since there were no leaves on the trees, from his living room I could see a wharf and across the harbor to the skyline of Boston.

"That's Tudor Wharf," he explained from where he was sitting, because even though he hadn't moved, he was obviously familiar with the view.

"Maybe I was looking at something else," I said, just to be contrary.

"But you're not."

Turning around, I crossed my arms as I regarded him.

"You have questions."

"I do. I wanna know what those guys told you."

"They said they were FBI agents and they were here to look out for me."

"And you told them about me? That I was coming?"

"Yes. I said that I would be fine because you were on your way."

"Okay, and what'd they say to that?"

"They said that when you showed up that I should tell you to go."

I nodded. "Did they show you their badges?"

He narrowed his eyes in thought.

I would have groaned, but that was rude. "Seriously?"

First he grimaced, followed it with a quick shrug, and then got up and walked over to just a few feet away from me. I was surprised when he raked a long glance up and down my frame, going so slow I couldn't miss his interest.

"Hey," I snapped, irritated that we hadn't met in some club where I could have done something about the attraction. I was working—I had to protect him—so throwing him over the table in his kitchen was out of the question.

"Sorry, what?"

The subtle pinking of his cheeks was very sexy. I had the nearly overwhelming urge to kiss him, and the desire was annoying the crap out of me—there was nothing I could do about it—so I barked at him instead. "You *always* ask to see badges."

"Do you? I mean, do most people do that?"

"Of course!"

"Yes, but that's sort of rude, isn't it? To question? To second-guess people? Starts you off on a bad foot, don't you think?"

"No, I don't," I replied tightly. "You should always ask. Any law enforcement officer expects you to, unless you're looking at the badge right out in the open."

He nodded. "Okay, I promise to check from now on."

God, he was cute. "With the chain on the door," I directed.

"Absolutely," he said, grinning at me. "So you were saying about being a bodyguard?"

But something hit me first. "I thought you were scared earlier, but you weren't, were you."

He scowled at me. "Why would I be scared? They were FBI agents."

"So then what was the problem?"

He bit his bottom lip and wouldn't meet my gaze.

"Brinley?"

"Brin," he corrected, his quiet focus on me for a second before it was gone. He visibly stopped himself from taking a step toward me. "Just… Brin."

"What was the issue, then, Brin?" I pried.

He raised his eyes, and I was swallowed in the sun-warmed brown velvet of his gaze. The comfort I saw there that he seemed so ready and willing to give made me clench my jaw. He was still, and I could not stop staring down at him.

"I didn't want you to go when I just got you here."

There was a story there. We had never met—as far as I knew—but he was acting like we had. Before I unearthed that mystery, though, I had to get him to understand his jeopardy. He had to be more ready and aware than he currently was.

I cleared my throat. "So they were here to kill you, right?"

"Who?"

"Those two guys."

"The FBI agents?"

I shook my head. "They were not FBI. I wouldn't have had to kill them if they were actually agents."

"Who were they?"

"I think they probably work for Anton Djordjevic."

"And who's he?"

"He's the guy currently having a turf war with my boss."

"Okay."

"Okay?" I rasped, getting agitated by how lightly he was taking his perilous position. "It's okay with you that you were almost killed?"

"I wasn't almost killed; you were here, so I wasn't really in any danger."

He was very dismissive of the threat to his life. "You're awful trusting."

"Are you or are you not my bodyguard?"

"Yeah, but that doesn't mean that you're not in jeopardy at the moment."

He appeared puzzled, the way his brows furrowed, which was ten kinds of cute, like a befuddled bunny, and his mouth quirked to the side.

"Are you listening to me?" I asked, starting to get worked up again. It was crazy. I was always calm, unflappable, but with Brin, looking at him, it was making me anxious. Already, so quickly, somehow, I was attached enough that I didn't want him to get hurt.

"Well, clearly, yes," he placated me, chuckling softly. "But I'm not understanding."

"I think you are."

"No," he breathed out, shaking his head.

"Those guys who I just took care of were here to end your life," I stressed to him, my voice stern, feeling my furrowed brows, the tension in my forehead. He was so delicate and sweet and… just thinking about him bleeding made my stomach hurt.

He crossed his arms as he stared up at me. "But really, that makes no sense."

"What?" Caught off-guard, my reaction, how big it was, and how surprised I sounded, annoyed the crap out of me. I needed to be steady, grounded, but for some reason he was screwing with my equilibrium. And yes, he was pretty—so very pretty—but beauty didn't normally throw me for a loop, so something else was going on.

"I'm not this important," he assured me, stepping closer, breathing in deep, inhaling my scent even as he reached out to touch the hem of my sweater.

I should have shoved him away from me or put some distance between us but... I couldn't. I didn't want to. Everything about the man was appealing. His smile, the curve of his delectable lips, the mischievous gleam in his eyes, the soft, sensual timbre of his voice, his long, thick lashes, and the husky sound of his laugh.

What the hell?

"I bet you're covered all over in muscle, aren't you."

"What?"

"You," he purred, "under those clothes... I bet you're yummy."

Yummy? The fuck.

"Do me a favor and siddown, willya?" I groused at him.

Without any further prodding, he walked back over to the couch and plopped down. I was going to take the wingback chair, but he patted the space beside him.

"I'll be good over here."

He shook his head, his eyes warm as he gazed at me.

Bewitching was the word that came to mind. For whatever reason, the man had me good and bespelled.

Once I took a seat, he turned so he could face me, folding his leg in half, sliding his knee along the outside of my thigh before he wedged his calf against me. I was going to move, give him room, but he wrapped his elegant long-fingered hand around my wrist and gifted me with me a sweet, reassuring smile, focused and ready to hear whatever it was.

"You're weird," I passed judgment.

"Or perhaps no one ever gives you their actual full attention. Did you consider that?"

I hadn't, no. "You don't look like a grad student," I said to try to break the spell he had over me.

"Oh?"

I shrugged.

"What do I look like, then?"

"I dunno." I had to think about it for a minute. "A rock star or something."

"Really?" His eyes lit up and the swirl of glittering gold in the sumptuous cognac was something to see. "What makes you say that?"

I gestured at him. "I don't expect smart guys to look like you." It sounded stupid, awkward, and I was talking out of my ass, but it was true. He was *not* what I'd been expecting, not the nerd I'd envisioned at all.

"In what way?"

"I don't—like your hair."

"What about it?" he teased.

"It's long."

"Longer than yours, yes," he agreed, "but I don't think anyone would let me in an eighties hair band."

They wouldn't, no. Up close, his hair was thick and glossy with just enough curl so it didn't hang flat. It was also wild and unruly, giving a hint about the man himself. He was not what I'd expected, not straight-laced, spoiled, buttoned-up, and buttoned-down. There was a winsome recklessness about him that needed to be protected.

"Ceaton?"

Annoyed by my reaction to him, I was gruff when I spoke. "Tell me what you're studying."

"Really?" The smile was infectious.

"Yes."

"I study lobsters."

There had to be more to it than that. And the fact that I wanted to know, that I cared in the least, was mind-boggling. I never delved, but for him I would.

"What?"

"I'm not stupid. You can say more than that."

"I would never think such a thing!" he announced as if I'd horrified him, clutching my hand, his expression all concern.

"Then," I prodded.

He cleared his throat. "Well, I study the effects of climate change on lobster diseases. For example, it could be that the bacterium that causes shell disease proliferates when waters are warmer. I look at the melting of arctic ice causing less mixing of oxygen and nutrients, especially low down in the water column, meaning less plankton, so less lobster food, and the lobster prey depend on that."

"Okay," I said, smiling at him, coaxing, nodding slowly and lifting my eyebrows. "And? Is there more?"

"You really want to… oh, okay." He coughed and flushed, and it was really cute. "Well, so, there's been work up in Maine on this issue, and I'm repeating that work further south."

"Right."

"Also, here, because there's trapping, the lobsters eat too much fish, which increases the bacteria they carry, so that causes them to get more diseases."

"And if the trapping areas have lobsters that are already stressed from that, then the climate thing might be even harder on them," I concluded, because it was the next logical step.

"Yes," he agreed, and I heard the sigh of pleasure. "I might swoon with you actually listening and having an opinion and following along."

"It's very impressive," I said honestly. "You're very impressive."

"I am?" he whispered.

"Very."

He caught his breath.

"Do you get paid to do this?" I asked, liking how his lashes fluttered when I took his hand in mine.

"I-I… do. This is grant-funded postdoctoral research."

"So you have your PhD already."

"I do."

"That's *really* impressive. How old are you?"

He cleared his throat. "I'm thirty."

"Are you really?"

"I don't look thirty?" He sounded breathless as he stared into my eyes.

"You look just barely legal."

"To drink or vote?"

I chuckled. "Drink."

"Oh thank God, I thought you were going to tell me I looked eighteen."

"Not quite that young, but it's better to look younger than older."

"Says the man who looks, what, twenty-five, I'm guessing?"

"I'm thirty-two."

"Perfect," he whispered, so I pretended not to hear it.

"Okay, now, listen—"

"You know when I went to have my tat done in California, no one in the shop asked to check my ID," he explained, taking off his sweater coat and turning to me, shoving the sleeve of his T-shirt up so I could see the tattoo that ran the length of his left arm from his shoulder to his wrist. "So I must have looked old enough to Ichiro Tokugawa, huh?"

"Who?"

"My tattoo artist."

Holy crap, my little PhD was just one surprise after another. First gorgeous and outspoken and not afraid to say what he wanted, and now, all tatted up.

It was gorgeous ink in black and gray, shaded and intricate, and stood out beautifully on his peachy skin with the flush of pale gold underneath. To see the entire thing, he'd have to take his shirt off, and since that wasn't going to happen at the moment—much to my regret— where he was holding the cotton sleeve up allowed me to view the head of a raven and its wing that, from the angle and the size of the bird, had to spill down across his chest as well as along his back. It was stunning, the attention to detail amazing, and I had to wonder how much time something so beautiful had taken. But I had to get him back to the task at hand, which was about him being vigilant.

"Brin, I need you to—"

"I want to talk to you, get to know you," he implored, his gaze on mine. "Just a little, just for a moment."

We'd be chit-chatting with bullets flying around us if I didn't get him focused.

"I really need you to—"

"Don't you want to know about the tattoo?"

I did, that was the problem.

"Oh," he gasped excitedly. "I saw that look, you *do* want to talk to me."

"I—"

"Just ask me," he pleaded.

Heavy sigh. "What's the raven about?"

"It represents thought." He beamed at me.

I nodded. "That's Norse mythology, right? Hugin is one of Odin's ravens."

"Yes," he said, grinning big. "And then underneath I have my Spartan."

The profile of a warrior was there on his arm, powerful, unyielding, in a helmet and cuirass, holding a spear, and I wondered what he was trying to evoke with that.

"I felt like," he began quietly, "I wanted to stay on the right path and not be distracted from my goal."

"Looking around this house, though," I mused, glancing around, "you're not missing a lot of creature comforts here, yeah?"

"Agreed."

"So then what's with the Spartan?"

"I think it's mostly a reminder to stay focused and serious."

"That makes sense," I agreed, "with all the studying."

"Yes."

"And then of course your lobster here on the bottom," I said, pointing, "which looks like one of those engravings out of a really old textbook or something."

"Which is exactly what it is," he mused, letting go of his sleeve, shifting closer to me as he put his arm back in his sweater and slipped it on. "I had the whole thing done when I got my PhD, and the lobster especially represented that achievement for me."

"Which is interesting because the tat doesn't seem doctoral at all," I said playfully, leaning back, getting comfortable… and then sitting up fast, rigid and straight. I had to be on guard—we weren't on a date.

"But this way I'm relatable to the students," he rambled on, ignoring my jolt.

"So is that the real reason you did it?" I asked, continuing the conversation, albeit more warily.

"No," he said, slipping his left hand over my thigh.

"No?"

"I got it because it was about me growing up."

"Oh?"

"What?" he teased. "You don't think I'm a mature, responsible person?"

"I dunno you well enough to say."

"That's fair," he conceded, lifting his other hand to my face, trailing his fingers along my jawline, delicately, reverently.

"How long did all that take to do?" I said, ignoring the fact he was touching me, unsure if asking what he was doing would elicit an answer or make him stop, neither being a good alternative. He needed protecting, which meant I had to be clearheaded, but getting him off me was not at all what I wanted.

He thought for a moment. "In total, twenty-four hours, but I waited a month between letting the raven heal and having the Spartan and the lobster done."

"The raven had to have been really painful with all the individual feathers."

"Yes, it was," he said with a sigh. "But there are more."

"What're you talking about?"

"There are more tattoos, just words, short phrases really, but I'd have to take off my clothes for you to see."

It was not professional in the least to tell him to show me—though neither was sitting down and chatting—so I swallowed the request as I turned toward him. The shift in my position wasn't big, but when I did it, he moved at the same time, drawing closer. I ended up with him almost in my lap.

The ripple of electricity that followed his motion started in my stomach and quickly spread to my chest and groin.

What in the world was going on?

Not once in my life had I reacted to anyone as I was reacting to Brinley Todd. I'd never gone breathless from a touch, never felt a tightening in my throat and a throb in my cock, had never once thought "I want to kiss this man and taste this man" with fucking being a hope and not a priority. Always, with me, if I was interested, it was to scratch an itch, not to spend time with someone, not to talk to or care for or discover. I'd wanted this, hoped for it, wondered if things like this even happened to real people, and now… at the worst possible time… I was faced with the realization that yes, it most certainly did.

"Fuckin' hell," I groaned.

"Pardon?"

"Just—"

"I don't like people in my personal space," he said by way of explanation.

He made no sense. "What?"

"It makes me nervous."

"So this is making you anxious, then?"

Quick shake of his head.

"Then why say anything?"

"So you'd know this isn't normal," he admitted before licking his lips slowly, then swallowing once, twice, as if he was gathering courage. "For me. This isn't normal for me."

"You too?"

He exhaled sharply, relieved, shoulders falling, smiling, pleased with me. "I like you."

"I like you too," I grudgingly admitted.

"Yeah?"

"Hard not to."

"Oh, that's good to hear."

"But see, I'm supposed to be guarding you, yeah? Not trying to figure out how I'm gonna get your clothes off."

"You don't have to figure that out. I'll just go ahead and take them off for you."

"That's not helping. And this is by far the weirdest conversation I've ever had."

He moved the lapel of my peacoat and pointed at the Sig. "The gun is hot."

"It's not. Even though I used—"

He snorted out a laugh.

"Oh." I was an *idiot*.

He waggled his eyebrows at me.

"You mean… shit… I know what you mean."

He laughed and, man, it was a good sound.

"Listen, I should—"

"Take off your coat and stay awhile?" he suggested, pushing it down over my shoulders. "Yes, I agree."

Not wanting to be tangled in my coat if someone came through the front door, I let him help me get it off and then watched as he folded it in half and draped it over the back of the couch before turning back to me.

"I'm worried that this—whatever's going on with us—is going to make you stupid and me slow, and I don't want that to happen."

"Okay," he agreed seriously. "How do you think we're going to get it?"

"What?"

"How will they attack us? Frontal assault?"

"Do you even know what you're talking about?"

"My guess is that they'll drive up in front of the house, right?"

"Yes. Probably."

"Okay, good," he said cheerfully. "Because from where we are, right here on the couch, we can see the whole yard and even out to the beach, so… we're good to go."

"Good to go for—"

He pressed me back into the couch as he crawled into my lap, straddled my hips, and stared down into my eyes.

"This is your idea of safe?" I asked.

"No," he mused, studying my face, seemingly drinking in the sight of me. "This is my idea of as good as it's going to get until this is over."

"And why do we have to settle for anything less than you being perfectly safe?"

"Because," he breathed, "you and I need to make with the dating already."

"Have you lost your—"

But before I could say any more, defuse the situation, get up, move away, or put some space between us, he took hold of my face, tipped my head back, and kissed me.

I was a scary man with a dangerous reputation, and normally the men I met were aware of that and enthralled. An aspect of being with me—I'd been told—appealed to the thrill seekers. When I walked into a bar or a club and men caught a glimpse of the gun in the shoulder holster, saw me shaking my hand with bruised knuckles, or stalked me into a quiet corner and caught me checking the knife strapped to my calf, they were enraptured by their own jeopardy. I was menacing, clearly able to take them apart but intent on seduction instead.

It was a rush, and I left when it was over and never, ever stayed, even when asked. I was the king of the one and done, and I always, without fail, initiated contact. Everything always happened on my terms. I was too big, too lethal for it to be any other way.

Until now.

Until this.

Until him.

His hands were clutched in my hair to make sure I wasn't going anywhere as he ground his mouth down over mine and slid his tongue along the seam of my lips until I opened for him.

A husky growl came up out of him as he got inside, notching our mouths together, wriggling against me until his groin was plastered to my abdomen—as close as he could be with his clothes still on—coiling his arms around my neck as he sucked on my tongue and tried to crawl down my throat.

He kissed the breath right out of me.

I had to get him off me, push him back, explain to him who and what I was, but never in my life had I tasted anything as sweet as the man in my arms. He drugged me, devoured me, and when he pulled back to take a gulp of air, I was leveled by the look in his dark eyes.

He didn't just want to fuck me; he was laying claim.

I should have run. I should have bolted out of the house and told Grigor to get someone else, no matter what Brinley wanted. He was obviously very confused about who I was.

"I know exactly who you are," he said, as if he were reading my mind, before he kissed me again, and I forgot why I was trying to get away.

Taking hold of his ass, I shucked him forward, unable to stop the roll of my hips, needing the friction, the grinding, my hunger for him like thunder in my blood.

I had no idea academics, scientists, could kiss like that. His mouth was hot on mine and he nibbled on my bottom lip, tugging just enough to get me to open so he could slip his tongue back inside, stroke, and tangle, and his low, greedy moan was very sexy when I had to pull back for air. He was trying to wriggle closer, and between the slumberous look in his eyes and his husky, whispered pleading, I was on the verge of taking him right there.

"Stop," I ordered, shoving him off me, trying to scramble off the couch, needing distance and air and my body under control.

Brin moved like an eel in my hands, twisting, pushing, taking advantage of me trying to get up as he was trying to shove me down, upsetting my balance so I ended up on top of him, my weight pinning him under me to the couch.

"Oh, this works," he purred, lifting to recapture my mouth, stealing my breath away with the force of his need.

I felt the kiss crackling its way down my spine, lighting me up, taking hold, and building an answering heat in me all over again. I wanted him badly.

"Come get in my bed," he rasped between kisses, hands all over me, burrowing one second, yanking the next, wanting me naked.

Taking hold of his face, I tried to break the kiss, but his teeth caught my bottom lip, so I couldn't. When I looked at him, he bit down harder.

I finally pinched his side, and he laughed and released me. Even though I tried not to, I ended up smiling down into the dancing brown eyes.

"You just attack any guy who comes into your house?" I accused him.

He shook his head even as he wiggled under me, arching his back, trying to get me to move between his thighs and not on top of them.

"Do you know who I am?"

"Yes." He nodded, eyes not on mine but on my mouth. "I know exactly."

I'd never been kissed like that in my life, and I really wanted to have it again, but I needed to get to the bottom of whatever this was.

"I need to talk to you, and if you keep touching me, I can't focus."

"I'm thinking that's not such a bad thing," he replied smoothly.

I tried to move, but he slipped his hands around the sides of my neck and slid a leg over my thigh. I'd have to hurt him to get him off me.

"Don't you think—"

"Give me your weight. Lie down."

He had no idea how much I wanted that. "You're distracting me," I muttered thickly, "and you're gonna end up getting hurt."

"The only one who can hurt me is you."

"That's a sweet sentiment, but that's not really the case."

"I beg to differ," he moaned softly, those dusky lips of his hard to keep my eyes off of. "Just lean a little closer."

I growled at him, and that deep, husky, decadent laugh made my dick throb.

"Oh, I felt that," he said, shivering. "You want me."

"I'd have to be dead not to want you."

And why in the world that made him giggle, I had no idea.

The pounding on the front door had me reaching for my gun as I remained braced above him on one arm. It couldn't be Marko and Pravi. They wouldn't knock. Someone else was on his front porch.

"Don't worry," he soothed me, whispering. "They're here for me, but they'll go away in a second. Just be quiet."

I checked him, and he was grinning and nodding as the knocking got more insistent.

"We know you're in there, Brin, and none of us want to go either, but this is for money, you piece of shit, so get the fuck out here!"

He groaned under me, and I couldn't help but smile.

"You're hiding from guys you know?"

"I'm not hiding," he said without making any noise.

I snorted out a laugh, shifting off him as he went limp in defeat under me. I got up from the couch, walked to the front door, and opened it.

Three men all took a big step back at the same time. They wore various stages of what I would consider dress clothes, but the combinations were strange. Like one was wearing a corduroy jacket with those suede elbow patches and a bow tie. One was in all black—suit, shirt, tie—which was a bit severe for four in the afternoon. And nothing fit well. The shirt was a bit snug, as evidenced by the pulling of the buttons, the tie was too wide, and the suit hung like maybe he'd borrowed it from his father. The last guy looked better than either of the other two, if not for the sweater vest under the suit jacket and the skinny tie with pink fish. They were an odd mix out there in the cold.

"Hi," Fish Tie said, looking me up and down. "We're here to see Brinley."

I moved so they could see inside the cozy seaside cottage.

"Go without me," Brinley whined from the couch. "I'll be right behind you."

"Bullshit," Father's Suit yelled. "Just because your research is funded doesn't mean the rest of us don't need patrons and donors, and you know as well as we do that everyone is supposed to be there!"

"I—"

"He needs to change," I interrupted before Fish Tie joined in the yelling. "And we'll be right behind you, I swear."

All three looked at me, took my measure, and then turned and clomped down the stairs, back out through the yard with the oak tree and the Norfolk pine and the big elm closest to the house. Closing the door, I turned around and saw the bemused smile on Brinley's face.

"Who the hell are those guys?"

He made a choking noise. "Grad students in my department," he explained, grinning at me. "They're more what you pictured, huh?"

"Yeah."

His wicked grin morphed into a full-on leer. "Come back over here."

"Nuh-uh, get up."

"They totally believed you," he said, ignoring me. "I've never gotten them to go away like that. I always end up having to—"

"We're leaving, come on."

Instant scowl. "No, no, no, I'm about to get laid."

"Is that right?"

He pointed at me. "You kissed me back."

I chuckled. "Yeah, I did. I shouldn't have, but I did."

"Yes, you certainly should have. You need to wrap your brain around being both protective and possessive."

"Do I?"

He nodded. "Yes. And I have faith in you. I think you're a multitasker. I could tell that about you right away."

"You could, could you?"

"Uh-huh. And I say you can take care of me *and* have me all at the same time."

Jesus, he was a handful. But I was already too far gone, far too enthralled to put on the brakes and tell him no. "Tell me you don't have a bodyguard kink."

"I don't have a bodyguard kink."

"Or a big guy kink."

He squinted at me. "I don't think that one's a thing."

"I think it is."

He shook his head and mouthed, *I don't think so.*

"Well?" I pressed.

He huffed out a breath. "No, Ceaton, I don't have a big beautiful man kink because ohmygod, that's just crazy. Who in the world would ever get turned on by a hard, muscular body and gorgeous blue eyes? That's just nutty."

"You know what I—"

"So," he hedged, biting his bottom lip. "Do you plan to kiss me again?"

"I dunno, you're gettin' awful lippy."

"Ceaton," he whimpered, "honey?"

Who was I kidding? "Yeah. I plan to kiss you again."

His breath caught and the smile was pure bliss. "How about now," he said, gesturing over his shoulder. "In my bed."

I put my hands on my hips, staring at him. "I am not this hot. What's up with you?"

"Oh, you're plenty hot, believe me."

I scowled at him.

He choked. "Do you—have you looked at yourself in the mirror lately?"

"Don't be stupid. I know what I look like."

"Clearly not," he teased, rolling to his feet. He charged around the couch to reach me and put his hands on my hips when he got there, then tilted his head back to meet my gaze. "I don't know who you've been hanging out with, but you are a very beautiful man, Mr. Mercer. And you're much more than just a pretty face."

"Oh yeah?"

He nodded.

"And how do you know this?"

"Because you were there on one of the scariest nights of my life, and you rode to the rescue just like every good knight in shining armor ever has."

"What're you talking about?"

He lifted up on his toes and gave me a quick kiss, just a brush of his silky lips over mine. "Do I get laid when we get home?"

"Don't change the subject. Explain what you just said."

"Okay, so we're skipping my mandatory social engagement?"

"No, you should do the things you always do."

"So we're going?"

"Yes, but—I want to hear about the worst night of your life."

"And I'll tell you, but maybe not right this second."

"Is that why?"

"Is that why what?"

"Are you grateful for something I did, and that's why you're all into me?"

If looks could kill….

"Sorry," I said, putting my hands up to ward off the death stare I was getting. "But you have to admit, that would make sense."

"It doesn't hurt that I know you're a hero down deep where it counts, but even if you were a prick, I'd still want to sleep with you."

"Oh, that's charming."

"Just stop trying to think of a reason for me to come to my senses. I like you, you like me, let's go from there."

"I wanna know about this incident. Tell me what happened."

"Like I said, if you'd rather talk than go see where I work, I understand."

I threw up my hands. "Now I'll feel like a dick if I don't go."

"Well, my colleagues *are* counting on you to get me there."

"I just—I want you to talk to me."

"And I want to talk to you."

We stood there staring at each other.

"I don't have to wait," I told him. "I could make you talk to me now." I sounded arrogant even as I bent to kiss him.

"You can make me do anything you want," he agreed, eyes on mine before his long, lush lashes fluttered shut as our lips met.

God, I was in trouble.

CHAPTER SIX

I STOOD there, waiting for him as I'd been asked, and watched him dart around his sweet little house before he disappeared down the hall.

It was a warm and welcoming little seaside cottage with rustic french country gray hardwood floors, built-in bookshelves in the living room, and antique hurricane lamps on both ends of the overstuffed couch with deep-button detailing. There were pillows and throws ready to lie down on or wrap up in, and the coffee table was cluttered with open books, a TV remote, and an iPod, as well as a magnifying glass and various maps. The Persian rugs that littered the living room were all in smalt and titian and damask that set off the distressed white walls, and a bay window looked out on a beach from the living room. I felt good in his house, relaxed, and since I was on edge everywhere, the feeling was at once completely foreign and frighteningly appealing. I was afraid I wouldn't be able to leave.

It was funny how the details of the space sort of crept up on me. I hadn't noticed much when Brin was in front of me. When he was in my space, he was all I saw, and for the bodyguard that I was supposed to be at the moment, that was the opposite of great. I needed to start noticing my surroundings immediately.

"Hey."

Looking over to where he stood, having returned to the living room from the hall, I found him hopping on one foot as he pulled on a pair of jump boots that were clearly not military issue.

"So this thing at the science center—it's not the open house because that was back in October. This is just my department, but I think since you're forcing me to go that you should have to suffer along with me."

"Of course I'm going with you."

"No, I know you're going with me, I get the whole bodyguard thing. What I'm saying is that you have to go as my date and be interactive."

"I can't do that. I'm there to protect you."

"I'd rather hold your hand."

"Do you get that people came to your house to kill you?"

He nodded.

"Then why aren't you taking this seriously?"

"I *am* taking it seriously."

"You're talking about holding my hand!"

"I thought we covered the part where you were a multitasker already."

"I can't protect you if we're on a date."

"I disagree and I have a question."

He was exhausting. "Go ahead."

"You're not normally a bodyguard."

"Yeah, I am. I guard my boss."

"That's not what I heard."

"Oh no?"

"I was told that you have people you oversee. You check on things and have other duties within Mr. Jankovic's organization."

"Right."

He shrugged. "So saying you're a bodyguard... that's not actually correct, is it."

And it wasn't, he was right. I hadn't been "hired muscle" in years.

"Don't get me wrong, I'm sure there is a protective element in your day-to-day duties, and clearly, by how easily you dispatched the two men who came to kill me, you're more than capable of being a bodyguard in the most basic sense of the word," he said, smiling at me, "but in all seriousness, don't you think you can kiss me *and* kill for me if the need arose?"

"I dunno. I hope I could, but you're really fuckin' distracting."

"That's marvelous," he uttered, sounding a little choked up as he pulled on his second boot before rushing over to me and leaping at the last minute.

I caught him easily, arms wrapped around him as he sighed happily before kissing me.

His tongue had already been tangled with mine more than anyone else's. He could not keep his hands and mouth off me, which I had to admit was a huge turn-on. Brinley being excited, happy, besotted with my company, showing me all his cards without fear, was a completely refreshing and a bit overwhelming experience. Game playing was a huge part of my life, but Brinley wasn't like that, not even a little.

"So where—" he said between kisses, "—are we on the promise to go to bed with me when we get home?"

I got my hands under his ass and lifted him so he could wrap his legs around my hips. "We need to talk a lot more."

He murmured something right before he cupped my jaw with both hands and laid a kiss on me that made my knees weak.

It was ravenous and mauling, and I tightened my hold on him because if I didn't, I'd put him over the back of the couch.

"Oh please," he moaned, breaking the kiss for air. "Ceaton."

I turned and knocked him back into the door, pushing up against him, squeezing his ass as he writhed in my hands, his kiss hungry and frantic, licking and biting, wanting more.

"Ceaton," he growled, skimming his fingers over my throat, my shoulders, exploring my body through touch, clutching, clinging, and grinding the erection I could feel through his layers of clothing into my abdomen. "Promise me you'll be mine."

Even that fast I knew he wasn't talking about just fucking. He wanted to keep me. That made zero sense, and my mind cleared and I tore free, putting him on his feet and pulling his hands free.

"You don't even know me," I barked, but it came out hoarse and broken.

He took hold of my face before I could brush his hands away and stared up into my eyes. "I know you and your heart, Ceaton Mercer. Don't think I don't."

It had to do with whatever had happened. That was what made him say such ridiculous things after having been in my presence for only such a short time. He'd made a judgment based on my actions at some specific place and time, and while I wanted to know when and what had transpired, it was clear that whatever had happened made me look if not godlike, then quite close to it.

"Ceaton."

My name tumbled from his kiss-swollen lips in a silky purr as he stood there in front of me with his tousled mane, liquid eyes, and rumpled clothes, all sweet and vulnerable, his face full of yearning and a deep flush on his cheeks.

It took everything in me not to grab him.

A heartbeat of raw, primal need coursed under my skin, and I knew, just looking at him, that my life would change if I just reached for him. I was comfortable with him, hot for him; I liked his voice, how his mind worked, and how he touched me, like I was precious and fragile and utterly his.

"What—" I coughed because my voice wasn't working. "—did I do for you?"

He opened his mouth to answer, but his phone rang at the same time. "Shit," he grumbled, walking to the end table by the door and picking it up. "This is not going to end until we go."

And since he'd already promised to share the details of whatever I'd somehow forgotten, I relented.

"We should go, then," I said, clearing my throat, trying to get my bearings, realizing a break from it being just the two of us was actually the best thing.

"I guess." He sounded resigned.

"Your people are expecting you."

He shook his head. "It's not a big deal."

"They made it sound like it was."

"Just because my boss said that he was going to feed me to the sharks if I missed another of these meet and greets doesn't mean—"

"He said what?"

He waved a hand dismissively. "Oh, he didn't mean it. He's a professor of molecular biology. If he really wanted me dead, he could think up a thousand more insidious ways to do it."

"That's not all that comforting."

"And besides, if he was going to use me for chum, it's more of a threat in the summer when there are actually sharks around here."

"I don't—"

"But I guess since you gave them your word, we really should go." He sighed dramatically. "I mean, really, it's just drinks and appetizers, and then we can either come back here and I can cook, or we can go eat in Lynn. I know the best place to feed you and get you liquored up so we can come home and I can take advantage of you."

I shook my head. "You're kind of incorrigible."

"Not normally," he replied, his tone different, implacable. "I have my work and my house, and now I have you here too. If I can keep you,

I'm set, so I'm going to do my damnedest to make that happen because I'm a good person and I deserve you."

"You're a good person, which is why you shouldn't want me, ya idiot." Jesus, how could anyone be so smart and so stupid at the same time? "No matter what happened with us, I'm not a good man."

"Says you."

"Says anyone who knows me!"

"Well, that hasn't been my experience."

"You—"

He grunted and reached for me. "Give me your hand."

I did without thought.

"I'm kind of excited now to show you my lab."

"Your what?"

"At the science center," he answered, tugging on my hand. "Hurry up."

I had no choice but to follow into the kitchen, out the side door that led to the garage. I took one look at the aqua blue Volkswagen Beetle with the white doors and stopped.

"What's wrong," he asked as he pushed a button on the wall and the garage door rose. It was odd, but I couldn't remember the last time I'd been in a one-car garage. It felt cramped and small. I was used to being in Grigor's five-car one.

"Come on, we gotta go," he prodded as he got in the car.

"How old is this thing?" I asked, walking to the passenger-side door.

"It's a 1958," he answered, starting the engine.

I opened the door and peered in at him. "I think we should take mine; I'm not gonna fit in here."

"Oh, you will too," he griped. "Just get in."

Having never been in a Beetle in my life, the curiosity factor kicked in, so I followed directions. I was a little cramped until I moved the seat back, and he reached over and patted my thigh before he pulled out.

"Christ, how is this still running?" I asked as he hit the remote to close the garage.

"They still make parts for it, and my mechanic works on Beetles," he said cheerfully.

We were quiet as he drove, and I had a couple of minutes to think as he made the quick right back out onto the main street.

"We could have walked," he said, making conversation as I looked at the ocean outside my window. "It's only ten to fifteen minutes away if we did that, but I thought if we wanted to eat after, then we didn't have to walk back home for the car."

He slowed as he passed through an open gate moments later, but there was no one in guard shack there.

"That's not very secure," I mentioned, not happy at all.

"Yes, well, we're pretty casual here at the MSC."

I'd noticed the NU sticker on his windshield. "So why do you bother having a current one of those?" I asked, pointing.

"Well, dear, if you park in here without one, they call the town cops, who will slap you with a fifty-dollar ticket."

"And the guard shack?"

"I'm thinking it's there for intimidation purposes only," he explained cheerfully. "By the way, that's Canoe Beach over on the left."

"I don't need a tour."

"Yes, but you should know where you are and your surroundings."

"I already mapped everything before I drove out."

"But it's not the same as seeing it and appreciating the scenery and learning about your new home."

I made a noise that usually scared people but just made him smile.

"Oh, that was adorable."

I terrified people. All the time. And I could hurt him, easily, but he was not afraid of me even a bit. It was confusing and exhilarating at the same time.

He parked and then turned to me. "I'm freaking you out. I can tell."

"Little bit, yeah."

"I'm sorry, my brain, I—I don't—" He thought for a moment. "—logical things don't mess me up, only things that make no sense."

"You *should* be a mess."

"Because of those guys, right?"

"Yeah."

"But I can see how that would happen."

"Guys coming to kill you, you can see why that would happen?" I asked, incredulous, because seriously, the man should have been a basket case. Or maybe he was, maybe this was how Brin handled stress and fear and panic. "Are you okay? Do you need drugs?"

"Listen," he began, taking hold of my left hand in both of his. "My father's an important man."

"Yes."

"So it makes sense that if someone wanted to put pressure on him to do something, that they would try and hurt me or his son or his daughter."

"Those are your siblings."

He shrugged. "They're related to me by blood, but I've never met either one of them."

"Really?"

"I'm illegitimate, right? They don't even know who I am."

"How can that be? The judge never told his family about you?"

"Nope, never."

If Brin were mine, if I were ever gifted with his permanent presence in my life, I would shout it from the rooftops. Everyone would know. How his father had not publicly claimed him—damn the consequences— years ago was beyond me. It took a moment for me to find my voice and when the words finally came, they were dark and brittle. "That's so shitty. I'm sorry."

He shrugged. "It doesn't matter. I never had any desire to know any of them."

"You never wanted to be rich?"

"I'm a scientist, man," he teased. "I just need grant money."

I laughed and his smile in response was big and beautiful.

"Where does your mother live now?"

"In Sedona. She has a store there. She makes these huge stained-glass windows that she installs in homes and churches and buildings all over the world."

"No shit."

He nodded.

"So where does your last name Todd come from?"

"From my father."

"You mean your stepfather."

"No," he corrected. "My mother married Desi Todd when I was three. He adopted me and raised me, so he is, in fact, my father."

"Desi Todd?" I teased him. "That's a fun name."

"Desmond," he said in a deep serious voice, arching an eyebrow for me. "Dad likes to be called Desi now that he's retired and doing his art."

I loved the impression he was doing of his dad; it was really cute. "His art?"

"Yes. He used to be a CPA, but now he makes this gorgeous jewelry that he sells for ridiculous amounts of money."

"Really." I'd always admired people who could do one thing their whole life and then change. It always seemed so hopeful.

He nodded.

"That's kinda neat."

"Right?"

"And they both live in Sedona."

"Yes. They have connecting galleries. His is called Timeless Creations, and hers is called Wanderlust. You can go on the Internet and look up their sites or go to their shops there in Sedona, which they may or may not be at, depending on if Mom is installing a window somewhere. Dad always goes along with her. He says it's important to show the other guys out there that she's taken so they don't get any funny ideas."

"Sounds like he really loves her."

"She loves him too. They've always been my ideal for what married life should look like. Relationship goals and all that."

"How did they meet?"

He snorted out a laugh. "She fell on him."

"I'm sorry?"

"She was getting off a bus, he was getting on, and she tripped and went flying through the air, and he caught her."

"That's kind of romantic," I said because, God, it really was.

"It's kind of klutzy, but if you knew my mother, you'd understand that it's par for the course. She can trip over a crack in the sidewalk."

I chuckled, imagining it, growing fond of her already. I had a sudden urge to meet her.

"She once fell over a fire hydrant and would have gone headfirst into crosstown traffic."

"Would have?"

"Dad caught her."

"Sounds like it's a full-time job for him."

"I would say so, yes," he mused, the softness in his voice in direct contrast to the heat of his stare.

"He never stood a chance, huh?" I said, trying to quash the flutter in my chest brought on by the possessive way he was looking at me, like I belonged to him.

"No. He never got on the bus after he caught her the first day. He stayed to talk to her, and they've never been apart a day since."

"That's very romantic."

"You think so?" he questioned. "She fell on him, and he took his opportunity and stayed. You don't find that opportunistic?"

"Sure, but why is that a bad thing?" I defended his father. "When life gives you a gift, you should take it."

"Oh?"

"Hell yeah." I was adamant, wanting him to see it from my side.

"Well, I happen to agree."

"You do?"

"Of course."

"'Cause your dad, I mean… he knew what he wanted."

"Yes, he did," he said, smiling, turning my hand over and lacing his fingers with mine. "We Todd men always know."

Wait.

"Always," he purred, eyes narrowed in half, and I felt like a mouse that had been caught gathering wool while the cat slipped around beside him.

"Brin—"

"I can't wait for you to meet them."

It was no use.

Whatever this was, however it played out, I was in. I was good and caught and probably had been from the second he tipped his head back and looked up at me. There was no use fighting, it was a fruitless struggle.

"You okay, honey?" he asked innocently.

My sigh was long. "So when did your mom tell you about the judge?"

"When it was time for me to go to college," he explained. "My folks made too much for me to get financial aid, but not enough to pay for everything, even with my many different academic scholarships. That's a tough spot to be in, and that's when she told me about the judge's money and who I was to him."

"Did you always know that Desi wasn't your biological father?"

"Yes. They told me as soon as I was old enough to understand."

"And were you okay with it?"

"Of course," he said matter-of-factly. "I know my father; I know he loves me. There's nothing that would or could change that."

"That's a lot of faith right there."

"Not really. I think most people just expect that of their parents. I've always trusted them to love me unconditionally."

He had so much faith in them, but it made sense. He already had so much in me. I'd never met anyone so hopeful and optimistic. "What about when you came out to them?" I asked, testing, wanting to know how deep their acceptance had run. "Were you worried then?"

"About telling my folks I was gay?"

"Yeah."

He squinted at me. "I never 'came out' and told them I was gay. I'd been talking about boys, kissing boys, having a husband since I was, what—six, I think. There was never a question of me dating girls or having a wife. I've always known, and so have they."

"Really." I was gobsmacked. I had no idea that people were actually like that. I'd always had to be careful of what I did and who I told. I couldn't even imagine growing up like Brin.

He nodded.

"That's kind of amazing."

"It's just my family."

"I think it's you, too," I apprised him. "I think you bring out the best in everyone."

"But you only get that way if you're taught and shown love and how to be compassionate to others."

I nodded because I suspected that was true.

"I'm guessing you didn't have that."

"You would be right."

"Well, that's all right," he whispered. "That's going to change now."

"You just believe that everything will always work out," I noted, curling a piece of hair around his ear.

"I do. So when they told me about the judge and the money, the only thing I was worried about was if it would change anything between them and me, and if the judge expected anything from me in return for the money."

"Like what?"

"I don't know, like, would he expect me to call him Dad or would I need to vacation in the Hamptons with him."

"Know a lot about vacationing in the Hamptons, do you?"

"I know it's where rich people go."

"I see."

He shrugged. "I just wanted to know if there were strings attached."

"But there weren't, and your folks promised nothing would change, so you took the money."

"I did."

"Do you still depend on the judge for anything?"

"Oh no, not for ages," he explained. "I got accepted to Berkeley for grad school on full scholarship, and from there to Northeastern for my doctorate."

"And now your work is funded by a grant."

"Yes."

"So everything is perfect."

"It is now," he said, lifting my hand and kissing my knuckles.

God, he was good for my ego. "Please tell me how you know me," I asked, holding his stare, wanting to hear the story.

He took a breath. "Come on, we need to get going."

"Brin!" I barked, frustrated, tired of the sidestepping.

"That was loud," he deadpanned, but before I thought to grab him and throttle him, he was up and out of the car.

Following fast, I caught up with him, grabbed his shoulder, and turned him around slowly to face me. "Talk to me *now*."

Sharp exhale of breath.

"Please."

"It's not that I don't want to tell you. It's just that I may or may not get emotional when I do."

I put my hand on his cheek. "I don't mind."

He shook his head slightly. "Okay, fine. You saved me," he announced, his voice gravelly and low.

Oh. It all made sense, then. He was grateful, and that was why he wanted to sleep with me. As a thank-you. "That's because I knew those guys were wrong as soon as I got here," I agreed, petting the side of his face, enjoying touching him. "But listen, I don't expect you to—"

"No." He shook his head, smiling up at me. "Not today, dingus."

"Whaddya mean, not today?"

"I mean, yes, you saved me today, but that's not why I wanted to see you. That's not why when I got the call from your boss that I insisted you be the one who had to come babysit me."

I waited.

"I feel so safe with you."

"Why?" This was the heart of the mystery and what I wanted to hear.

"First you have to move your hand because the heat from your palm is distracting."

I let my hand drop but continued to stare at him.

"We have to go over to the main research building, all right?"

"Sure."

"So," he said as we began our walk. "I have a friend, Laine Woodgate, and he had a boyfriend that used to knock him around."

"Okay," I said as I shortened my steps so Brin could easily keep up.

"And the first time it happened, this guy, Archie Beale, he apologized up and down and sideways and said it would never happen again."

"It always happens again."

"I know. That's what I said," he assured me, slipping his hand into mine. "I said, 'Laine, he hit you once, he'll hit you again,' but he wouldn't listen."

I nodded, liking the fact that even though, apparently, me touching him was a distraction, he was the one initiating contact again. It was warm, connected. I felt like there was only the two of us. "Go on."

"Well, so I begged Laine to get away from the guy, but he didn't, of course. He just kept forgiving him, and of course it escalated until finally Laine broke it off and came to live with me after Archie beat him so bad that he put him in the hospital."

I tensed, and he made a sound implying that reaction was good and squeezed my hand tighter.

"The whole time the abuse was happening, everyone saw it. Nobody gave a shit, not his parents, not his brother, nobody, not even the police—no one until you."

"Me," I said, stopping, staring, not surprised that I was in the story but caught by surprise over the timing.

He rounded on me. "Yes, you."

"What're you talking about?"

Easing his hand from mine, he took a step back, holding my gaze the whole time. "Two years ago me and Laine were at a diner in Mission

Hill around two in the morning, and when we were on our way out, his ex-boyfriend—very much ex by that time—was there waiting for us."

I stayed quiet, not wanting to interrupt him.

"Archie grabbed Laine and pulled him around back, and I ran after them and got out my phone to call 911, but when I turned the corner, Archie was waiting and he punched me in the face, and when I fell, he took my phone and stomped the shit out of it."

I needed to hear this whole story. The waiting was twisting my stomach into knots.

"Laine ran, and I don't blame him. I mean, he had just gotten out of the hospital that day, and suddenly he was back in the nightmare."

"So he left you alone with his homicidal ex?"

"Yes."

Jesus. "There's never a reason to run away and leave your friends."

"That's not fair to say."

"The hell it's not!"

He shook his head. "Not all of us are big and strong, my darling. Some of us, when it's fight or flight, the flight is what kicks in."

"Still," I said curtly, angry for him, and then I caught my breath as my memory kicked in and I remembered the parking lot he was talking about. "Oh shit."

His grin was instant and brilliant. "Do you remember that now?"

I did.

It had been one of those weird nights in January, cold as hell but rainy instead of snowy, so when it stopped, there was still so much cloud cover that it wasn't dark, but a deep, light- sucking charcoal. It was dim outside, shadowy, the perfect night for vampires and werewolves and other predators.

I'd been sitting there eating, alone for once, having just left Marko and the others, when I saw a man dart across the street. The way he did it, the way he moved, caught my attention: skulking, careful, having checked both ways before he ran, which made no sense on a deserted street in the predawn hours. There was a short list of reasons for that much looking around, and they usually started with either being scared, or the flip side, afraid of getting caught making someone scared. Either way I had to know. It was engrained in me to always go with my gut, follow up on anything out of the ordinary. Something simple could blow up in my face if I disregarded my instincts.

When I moved quietly around the back of the diner, maneuvering in and around the huge oaks lining the parking lot of the neighborhood eatery, I saw a man—who I now knew to be Archie Beale—using his right fist to pummel another—who I now knew to be Brin.

"You think you could keep him from me, you fuckin' piece of shit?"

Brin gagged and choked on the blood filling his mouth.

"I told you what would happen. I told you what I would do," Archie snarled, hitting him again before yanking him around the side of the dumpster and flipping him to his stomach.

I heard the switchblade as I closed in on them, but I didn't see it. There was no moonlight to glint off the metal.

Brin vomited blood beneath him before Archie shoved his face down in it and lifted his ass in the air.

"You make one more sound and you're dead," he threatened Brin as he yanked his pants roughly down his thighs.

There was no question that I was going to intervene; I had already decided on a course of action, but when I saw all that Archie intended, I saw red.

He was going to rape Brin. He was going to teach him a lesson by violating him. Because he was bigger and stronger, because he'd apparently threatened it, for those reasons he was going to follow through on the promise.

"No," Brin whimpered beneath him, struggling to move, clawing at the hard ground. "Get the fuck off me!"

Archie was big compared to Brin, massive, at least six four, but I had muscle on him that I used to my advantage, as well as advanced training most guys on the street did not possess. Rushing up on him, I kicked him squarely in the side, which knocked him into the dumpster, clunking his head against the solid steel in the process.

Bending over, I picked up Brin, who still had his head down, moved him off to the side in the wet grass, and then rounded on Archie.

He was just climbing to his feet when I charged back, thinking I would pull the KA-BAR I always had strapped to my calf but realizing instantly that there was no need since he had no idea how to use his own knife. Clearly, he wasn't trained, didn't even know how to hold his weapon correctly, so I grabbed his wrist, wrenched it back, heard it snap, and then when the blade fell, kicked it underneath the dumpster.

As he howled over the pain, cradling his broken limb, I punched him square in the jaw.

"You fuck!" I roared, catching him before he fell, spinning him in my arms to deliver the sledgehammer blow to his kidney.

His cry of pain was loud but muffled because, halfway to his knees, I caught him in the nose with one of mine. He went down hard, face first into the asphalt, out cold.

When I finally turned to look for Brin, he was gone. I heard sirens in the distance that I knew would be for me if I didn't get out of there. But even then, I walked over to where I'd laid him down and stepped farther into the bushes to check, but to no avail. He was nowhere to be found.

"I looked for you," I rasped, reaching for Brin in the present.

He let me draw him close as his eyes filled, and I cupped his face in my hands. "I thought he was going to kill me, and then I was sure he was going to rape me. He was so mad, so full of hate, blaming me for everything, and he had that knife."

"He had to have been stalking Laine, right?" I asked gently, brushing away his tears.

"Yes."

"I'm so sorry. I wish I had gotten there sooner."

"Are you kidding?" He sniffled but his voice, even nasally, was full of wonder. "You should have your own theme music! You were amazing."

"I was late, was what I was," I muttered angrily.

"No!" he yelled, surprising me with how adamant he was even as the tears continued to roll down his cheeks. "You saved my life! And I know it's getting to be a thing with you since you did it today, too, but that night… ohmygod, Ceaton, where did you even come from?"

"I was inside," I explained, stroking his cheeks, swiping at the tears under his eyes. "And I noticed Archie and he seemed sketchy, so I went to check it out."

"Thank God you did." His head bumped against my chest as he shuddered.

I hugged him tight, clutching at his back and his hair, as he relived it and broke down sobbing, his face buried in my sweater.

I'd taken many beatings like that in my life, both the one Brin had endured and the one I'd given Archie, but I'd never, ever, threatened or been threatened with rape. That was something I couldn't even imagine. That brand of violence was beyond my comprehension.

It was the same reason I'd insisted on Grigor getting out of the prostitution business all those years ago. I couldn't allow others to be violated on my watch. If I could do something about it, I would. It made me sick to my stomach to even imagine.

I held him for long minutes until the sobs lost force, quieted as bawling became crying and then that halting, intermittent catching of breath before soft weeping.

I curled around him, tightening my hold, kissing his hair, his temples, rubbing circles on his back, all the while telling him I was there and so was he and that it was over.

"It's done," I promised, trying to draw the fear and sadness out of him and into myself, thrilled to feel him squirm to get loose enough he could wrap his arms around my neck and hold on.

We stood there together in a cocoon of warmth and comfort until I heard him inhale deeply and then let it out, slow.

Stepping back, I was gifted with a radiant smile.

"Is there Kleenex in the car?"

He nodded, voice still not quite working, and I dashed back to the car and found the package of tissues in the small glove compartment. Grabbing several, I returned quickly to him.

"Blow," I ordered.

He grinned up at me through the last of the stray tears—God, he was beautiful—and then blew his nose several times. When he was done, he wadded up the tissue and shoved it in the pocket of his field jacket before looking up at me.

I brushed the hair out of his face and then bent and kissed his forehead. "Can you tell me what else happened?"

He swallowed and took a breath, and when he spoke it was croaky before it evened out. "It took me a few minutes, but I got up and went to the back door of the diner and scared the shit out of the cook."

"I bet you did."

He nodded. "Yeah, so, he took me out front and they called the cops."

"That's good."

"I didn't want to leave you because Archie was so big, so I stayed to make sure you'd be okay, but when I saw you break his wrist, I figured you had him."

"I did."

"You were gone by the time the police got there, and I was sorry about that. I wanted you to get a medal or something."

"No, they would've charged me with battery, I'm sure."

"I wouldn't have let them," he promised, his bottom lip quivering.

I smiled at him. "Did you see the knife go under the dumpster?"

"Yeah. I told the police about it, so they found it and took it in as evidence."

"And what happened to Archie?"

"He was charged with stalking and threatening Laine, and with beating me up. They couldn't charge him with attempted rape because there was no evidence."

"I'm sorry they couldn't add that charge."

"No, you don't get to be sorry for anything. You were my miracle."

I swallowed around the knot in my throat.

"You broke his nose, you broke his jaw, and you broke his wrist. The police detective told me that Archie was lucky to be alive. He said that the beating was so brutal that whoever did it had to be trained in hand-to-hand combat."

"Huh."

"Were you a soldier?"

"I was a Marine."

Quick breath. "Well, so before I got the restraining order, I went to see Archie in the hospital, and I told him if he ever came near Laine or me again, that you would put a bullet in him, no questions asked."

"But you had no idea who I was."

He shook his head. "No, but he didn't know that. I told him you were new in my life, my boyfriend, and that he should steer clear."

"And did he?"

He nodded. "Oh God, yes, I've never seen him again. Laine heard he moved to Phoenix after he was released from jail."

"Good."

"Yes, it was," he exhaled, and I saw the last of the tension leave him.

"I don't understand. You said Laine went to the police and they didn't help him?"

"No. I went with him, and no one gave a damn."

"Why not?"

"Do I really need to say?"

"Please. Enlighten me."

He shrugged. "I think it's the gay thing."

"What does that mean?"

"I think they thought the same thing his father and brother and everyone else did, that when he said his boyfriend was abusive, that he could handle it."

"Yeah, but he went to them for help."

"He did, yes, but the first cop he ever gave a statement to said, 'But you're a guy and he's a guy—can't you two just work it out?'"

I bristled, feeling the anger take firm hold of me. "Well, I dunno how big Laine is, but that guy Archie was a helluva lot bigger'n you," I ground out.

"Everyone's bigger than me," he teased.

"Fine, but that guy Archie was taller than *me*."

"Yes, but you're way more built, whole lot more muscle."

There was that. "I just don't get it. Did Laine never take this Archie to meet his folks?"

"He did."

"But then they would have known that he never stood a chance if it got physical."

"I don't know what they did or didn't think, but Laine told me that his father thought he should have been able to handle it because, again, they're both guys."

"I'm sorry," I said sincerely, wanting to ease the pain for him.

"It's the same double standard he got from the police," he ranted. "I bet you if Laine were a girl, they would've locked his ex up and thrown away the key!"

"Sadly, I don't think—unless a murder's been committed—that the cops ever throw away the key on an abuser."

He thought about that for a moment. "Well, I'd lay odds that Laine's father would have gone after Archie with a gun *if* Laine were a girl."

"Maybe," I conceded, "and maybe not. Depends on the type of man he is. Me, boy or girl, it wouldn't matter. I'd be the kind of father who takes out your lungs if you touch my kid."

He sighed deeply. "Yes, I know."

I raked my fingers through my hair, frustrated with the entire story. "I'm so sorry. I wish I could've stopped it sooner."

"Please," he said, putting a hand on my shoulder. "The second you saw him hurting me, you acted. I couldn't ask for a better protector."

It made sense. "So when you saw me at the party—"

"I recognized you immediately, and I was so stunned I walked into the pool!"

"Jesus."

"What?"

"Grigor thought something different."

"Oh?"

"Yeah," I said, chuckling. "He thought you were overcome with lust."

"Oh, I was that too."

"No, it was gratitude then, and it's—"

"Listen." He stressed the word. "You saved me. I mean, you were amazing and heroic and I was overcome and thankful and everything else, but seeing you again filled me with lust, not gratitude."

I snorted a laugh.

He clutched my hand tight and put his other on my cheek. "I have dreamed about you a hundred times and wondered about you more times than I can count. When I saw you at the party—I couldn't believe it was you. I nearly swallowed my tongue."

"I—"

"You have to know, Ceaton Mercer, you're simply breathtaking."

I had no idea what to say. The most radiant creature I'd ever seen in my life was telling me he thought *I* was beautiful. It was a bit overwhelming. "Who told you my name?"

"Your friend."

"My friend?"

"Luka, I think his name was."

Holy shit. "When the hell was this?"

"That day at the party."

Shit, I had forgotten all about the Fourth of July.

"Are you all right?"

"I'm—" I was flustered was what I was. "But you pretended to ask my boss my name today."

"Yes. I didn't want to get your friend in trouble for talking to me."

"You're very smart."

"I try."

I nodded. "So what now?"

"Well, now, if it would be okay, I'd like to spend a lot of time with you."

"Baby, we're gonna be together night and day until I'm sure you're safe."

"And after that?" he prodded.

"Listen," I began. "Now that you told me the whole story, I get why—"

He scoffed. "Please stop. I was never grateful."

"Yes, you were. I saved your life," I contended, my voice rising.

"You did save my life," he agreed, "but that's not why I want to spend time with you."

"Then what is it?"

"Well, clearly you can't see this, but you're beautiful and sexy, you have a heart of gold under all those muscles, and I can already tell you're possessive and passionate just by how you've been in the last few hours."

"You make me sound a little scary."

"Which you are, but not to me."

"Maybe I should just focus on protecting you for the time being."

"You can do that too," he said, stepping in close to me, knocking his head on my chest, and wrapping his arms around my waist. "Just as long as you can do it sleeping next to me."

I tried not to rest my cheek on the top of his head, or enfold him into a hug, or feel so content and grounded when I did either of those things. I really did. But he was already under my skin, and having him close was having a soothing effect on me.

I could get used to having him around really easily.

"When I got the call this morning and your boss said that you could come out here and be my bodyguard—" A whimper came from the back of his throat. "I thought I was dreaming."

Slowly, gently, I took his face in my hands and tipped his head back so I was looking down into all that bottomless mink brown. "You don't owe me anything."

"I know that," he said, slipping his hands around my wrists, staring into my eyes. "But so you know—all I've wanted for the past two years since I moved here to Nahant was to find you and get you into my house and into my bed."

I let him go and took a step back. "You don't know anything about me."

"The hell I don't," he said, following right behind me.

Bolting forward, I darted around the side of a parked Mini Cooper. I had to try again to make him see the truth. He deserved better, and even though I very much wanted to be the new guy in his life, it wasn't fair to him. What kind of future did I truly have to offer? More danger? More chances to be killed? I was a bad choice from the start. "I'm not a good man."

"Oh no?" he baited me, slipping around the car.

I scowled at him as I moved, making sure I kept the car between us, feeling a little stupid but needing his hands off me so I could think. "Let me remind you that I kill people."

"Yeah, bad people, I know," he said, trying to get to me.

Apparently I was faster than he thought, and his growl of frustration was really cute. "They're not all bad," I informed him.

"What?" He wasn't really listening, too caught up in the chase.

"The people I kill," I reminded him. "They're not all evil."

"Is that right?" he said, arching an eyebrow. "Gunned down a lot of grandmothers, have you? Kids? Pregnant women?"

"God no." That was horrifying.

"Uh-huh," he said like he was bored, even as he slid around the front end of the car. "And the men you've killed, they've all been pillars of the community, right?"

I was going to stand my ground, but the way his eyes glinted and the way he bit his lip that made his dimples pop, I knew I was in trouble, so I bolted around to the trunk. "A few of them were probably good men."

"Who just so happened to be in business with the Serbian mob."

I froze. "How the hell do you know about the Serbian mob?"

He tipped his head sideways. "So I what? Live in a bubble? I don't read the news, the Internet is a new and mysterious thing?"

"What did you do?"

"I googled Grigor Jankovic back when he first invited me to his house for a party on the Fourth of July."

The party again.

"And when my father said, oh, Grigor will send someone out to protect you, that's how I knew to ask for you."

Fuck.

"I know all about the backdoor dealings my father has with your boss."

"Oh yeah? Who told you all that?"

He arched an eyebrow and waited for my brain to start working.

"Fuckin' Luka," I grumbled.

"Oh, look how big your eyes got!" He cackled.

"For crissake, how long did you guys talk?"

"Quite a while," he placated me. "He explained everything to me."

Of course he had.

"In lavish detail."

Good God.

"Just a regular fount of information, that one."

Talking to strangers: that was exactly what you wanted from the guys in your inner sanctum if you were a mob boss.

"He was hammered, by the way," he said with a wicked grin. "And very chatty. I wanted to know all about you, and though he was careful about that and wouldn't tell me much—" he sighed his approval, "—really good friend you have there by the way—he did not miss telling me anything about my father and your boss."

"Jesus Christ, I'm gonna kill him."

"Why?"

"Why?" I yelled, indignant. "Because he could have put you in danger! He could have put himself in danger! For fuck's sake, you don't tell a complete stranger your fuckin' business."

"Yes, but I wasn't a stranger. After I got out of the pool, your boss had me use his shower, and he got me some clothes to wear and introduced me to everyone as the judge's son."

"That was a power play on his part, right?"

"Course."

"He shows you around, lets anyone and everyone know that he's in so tight with the judge that his kid hangs out at his place."

"Pretty smart," Brin reasoned, inching closer to me. "But back to you, Ceaton Mercer."

"Listen, you—"

"Stop moving and let me put my hands on you."

I pointed at him. "You're just turned on by danger. You're an adrenaline junkie."

He shook his head. "Nope. I actually hate anything remotely scary. I'm a biologist. I like things orderly and calm and filed by genus."

"Then what's with you wanting to fuck me?"

He jolted as though startled. "I have no interest in fucking you."

Now I was surprised. "Liar! You just said—"

"I want to take you to bed and make love to you and then sleep with you after," he explained, his voice silky and low as he came closer, stalking me. "And then when we wake up, I'll feed you and then we'll make love all over again, and somewhere in there between the eating and the sleeping and the sex, you'll see how well I can take care of you, and you'll decide to stay here and live with me."

He was insane. "You have lost your mind."

"Why?"

"You can't want me." I was indignant. "I'm not a good man."

"You keep saying that. Are you trying to convince me or you?"

"I just killed two guys and put them in your toolshed," I recapped.

"Well, as you said earlier, where else would you put them? You couldn't very well leave them on the front lawn for the neighbors to see."

"You're really weird," I snapped at him, not even sure what I was saying, he had me so rattled. Between him knowing about Grigor and who I was and what I did and being okay with me killing people but still thinking I deserved to be loved… I was in over my head.

He threw up his hands. "I'm a scientist. I'm very logical."

"The words coming out of your mouth are not logical, believe me."

"All right, fine, look at it from my side," he coaxed as he stepped in close, having gotten the jump on me when I was thinking about him being nuts. "You protect Grigor, you saved me—twice now—and you're really great at spotting bullshit. Shouldn't I want someone like that around? Does that not make sense?"

"I—"

"Just stop," he soothed, reaching up to take my face in his hands. "Please. Turn your brain off and just come with me and let me show you where I work, all right? I want to share it with you because I'm crazy about you, and I think you could be crazy about me too if you just let yourself try."

There was no need to try. I was interested, no issue.

"So," he said seductively with that grin that made my heart race, "will you let me show you around?"

"I just—you should—"

"Breathe," he commanded with a chuckle. "Come on, baby, just breathe."

My groan was loud.

His giggle was evil.

"Sure. Fine. Whatever." There was no use fighting him. I couldn't win, mostly because I didn't want to. Yes, he came on like a hurricane, but I didn't want to seal myself up away from him either. I wanted his brand of crazy in my life.

He was pleased, and his creamy gilded skin pinked up as he took my hand and led me where he wanted me to go, pointing things out like the lab buildings, the main research structure, and the classrooms, a test pool for undersea robotics, a greenhouse, a tank farm with marine life samples, and then the back of the property with public hiking paths around East Point. It was a beautiful facility, and his pride in showing it to me was obvious.

Inside, behind the aquatics room, he took me into his office and lab. "Isn't it great?" he asked excitedly. "This is where the magic happens."

"Oh yeah, you've got all the bells and whistles in here."

His smile was wicked. "Don't make fun of me."

"No," I teased. "I love the stapler."

He bumped me and then showed me everything in the room from his maps to his collection of antique bookplates from 1852, his framed Gyotaku lobster print he got in Japan, and the many different specimens of dead lobsters. He held them and explained what I was looking at, and I listened because it was as important to him as how being able to shoot a McMillan TAC-338 rifle was to me.

I would have to get my CheyTac M200 as well as my Timberwolf C14 out of storage to show Brin.

The thought was sobering. I was planning to include him, to show him things it had never even crossed my mind to share with anyone else.

"Are you okay?" he asked, interrupting my thoughts.

"Yeah, why?"

"Well, you were smiling, and then all of a sudden, you looked sad."

"No, no, I'm good. I was listening," I said quickly.

"Yes, I know you were, but you were gone for just a second there."

I squinted at him. "This might sound weird."

"I love weird," he promised.

"You're really passionate about this stuff, and I'm really passionate about my guns and what I can do with them."

"That gun?" he asked, tipping his head at the holster under my coat.

"My rifles," I explained.

"Oh" came his response, and the way he said it, the way he perked up, eyes widening, newly alert, excitement on his face, made me realize he wasn't screwing around. He was interested in this topic. "Would you teach me?"

I scrutinized him. "You want to learn to shoot?"

"Not at animals or people or anything, but I always wanted to be able to shoot a target from a distance or be able to shoot skeet like rich people do."

I chuckled.

"What? It's a life goal."

"Okay, then."

"Excellent," he concluded, beaming at me but also tipping his head, scrutinizing.

"Something else?"

"I should ask you the same. Was there another thought in there along with the guns? Because your smile changed, like I said."

"I just—I've never wanted to show anyone else before."

"And you were concerned about what that means."

"Yeah," I replied softly.

"I think it means that you're open to the possibility of us spending time together, and to me—that's wonderful news."

"It's… weird."

"What is?"

"You."

"We've covered that, haven't we?" He chuckled, staring at me like he was drunk. It was really heady stuff, to be stared at like I was a dream come true. I could get used to it.

"No, I mean you're acting like I'm some kind of prize and it's weird for me."

"Well, get used to it," he sighed. "Because it's never going to change."

Never. As in for the rest of my life. "Do you hear what comes out of your mouth?"

"Of course. Now come on, I have to show you off."

"Pardon?"

I got a really cute eyebrow waggle in response and realized whatever he wanted, I would do. It hardly mattered what it was or where we went. I would have missed the bus, too, just like his father did with Brin's mom.

ONCE WE entered the main building, Brinley led me down a long hallway, and at the end we emerged in a larger room where a string quartet was playing. There was a bar on one wall and waiters walking through the crowd with appetizers.

"I'll get us some drinks," I offered, leaving him talking to the three men who were at his front door earlier. When my phone rang after I ordered a couple of Rieslings, I checked the number and picked up.

"Where are you?" Pravi asked.

"At a science mixer."

Nothing.

I couldn't stifle the chuckle.

"Tell me again," he demanded.

"You heard me," I said, grinning. "Brinley and I are having drinks at the marine science center just down the road. I can be back there fast if you need me."

"No. We found what we were looking for."

"I figured you would."

"But we forgot the food, so we have to go pick some up. We'll be back later."

"Sounds good," I agreed and was about to hang up because that was as much talking in code as we needed to do.

"I need you to ask Brinley a question," Pravi said unexpectedly.

I cleared my throat. "You wanna text me?"

"No, it's okay. I just needed to know if he received a package today."

"It's Sunday."

"It didn't come in the mail."

"Okay. Do you know who the package is coming from?"

"Yes. His father."

"All right, well, lemme ask and I'll call ya right back."

"Good."

Taking the two white wines, I made my way over to Brinley, who was now in the middle of about ten people all listening as he explained about his research. They were riveted as he waxed on about bacteria and trapping and then about lobster-pot poaching—which I would have to ask him to clue me in on later because apparently it was a federal offense—and how progress was not going well in regards to setting fishing limits on local fishermen.

"Hey," he breathed when he noticed me, taking the wineglass I offered him before he slipped his arm around my waist and leaned. "I wanted to introduce you to everyone."

Clearly, from the interest I was getting, he was important to a lot of these people: the head of his department and advisor, Ethan Park; his teaching assistants—because apparently Brin taught as well—and more colleagues, including a guy who could not stop scowling at me, another colleague who just returned from Antarctica, and another who was leaving for Bolivia in a few days who needed Brinley to teach one of his classes at the college.

Everyone except the guy who clearly wanted me dead was pleased I was there with Brinley. Once I was done smiling and shaking hands, I excused us for a second.

"Are you ready to go?" he asked, putting a hand gently on my chest.

"When you are. I'm not in any rush," I assured him. "I just needed to know if you got a package today."

"No, I don't think so, but it's Sunday, right?"

"Yeah, I know, that's what I said, but one of the guys I work with just asked me."

"That's strange."

It was, actually.

"Did he say who the package would be coming from?"

"Yeah, the judge."

"Huh."

"What?"

"Just, I've never gotten anything from him in my life, so it would be really odd if he started sending me things now."

"What about money?"

"No. When I received my funds from him, I just went to the bank and signed a card and took over the account. I just had to show the bank who I was."

"So then getting anything from him would be really out of the ordinary."

"Yes, it would," he replied, slipping a hand up under my sweater to my skin. "But I haven't received a package or any other kind of correspondence from him, and I really have no interest in him at all. The only thing I care about at the moment is that because he was scared for me, he called your boss, and poof... here you are."

I smiled down at him, carding my fingers through his hair, loving the silky feel of it on my skin. "Poof?"

He murmured something I missed, but the contentment on his face told the tale. He was very pleased to have me there, happier than he should have been.

"I'm trouble, you know."

"Mmmm-hmmm." He wasn't listening.

"You need to understand that—"

"You're wonderful, and us, being together, is fate."

"That's not—"

"Yes, it is true," he crooned.

"No."

"Yes. Oh very much yes."

"Brin."

"We're soulmates."

"Oh yeah? How so?"

"Think about it. Our lives not only intersected once, but twice. What are the chances?"

"I—"

"How is that anything else but fate?"

"True," I agreed huskily, liking the quiet little bubble we seemed to find ourselves in. He had a really soothing, grounding effect on me that had been completely missing in my life up to this point, and I really wanted to spend a lot more time with him.

"I mean, we're supposed to be"—he gestured back and forth between us—"together."

"Oh yeah?"

He nodded. "Yes," he said adamantly. "Just looking across the room and seeing you waiting to get my drink for me, I was filled with this overwhelming feeling of rightness."

I should have been scared. It was way too fast. And he wasn't talking about love, but he was saying we needed to be around each other all the time, sharing space, and to not be separated, and who did that? Who jumped into anything that quickly?

"I want to look at you for the rest of my life."

"You get how nuts you sound, right?"

He nodded.

"And you're sure this isn't gratitude or anything else?"

"I am."

"So what, then?"

"I just…. I feel like when you walked through my front door, there was a shift in the axis of my life, like the rings of Saturn, like a tilt."

"What?"

"There was a pushpin in my mind map of where I thought I was, but you moved it, you changed it, and now my orbit is different because of you."

"Do you even know what you're saying?"

He set his glass down and then took mine and did the same before leading me quickly away from the rest of the crowd to the other side of the room where it was quieter.

When he rounded on me, I saw the intensity on his face, how he was searching my eyes even as he maintained eye contact. "You saved me, right?"

"I did, but—"

"I think I'm supposed to save you right back."

CHAPTER SEVEN

WE EXCUSED ourselves from the mixer. We were both starving, he'd put in his time, and, as he explained, he was going to basically be useless until he got in some alone time with me. Halfway to the car, we were stopped by the guy who'd been giving me the death stare ever since we'd walked in, and I waited as Brin talked to him.

When he joined me a few minutes later, he told me to get in the car, which I did without question. He looked strange, a little flustered, even more annoyed as he started driving, and I was going to wait and let him explain himself, but I blurted out the question instead because my impulse control was apparently nonexistent where he was concerned.

"Who was that guy and what the hell did he want?"

"I introduced you inside," he said. I understood, just from the time we'd spent together, that giving the logical answer was his default.

"Yeah, I know his name is Owen Stewart. I just don't know what the hell he wanted," I grumbled, more irritated than I had a right to be.

"Well, what he wants is me, apparently."

"Sorry?"

"Back."

"Back?"

"Yes. He's my ex."

"And what did you tell him?"

The noise he made was a scoff and a snort with a healthy dose of disgust thrown in for good measure. "I told him that his timing was terrible, and that he'd been my ex for the better part of a year now, and that if he thought I was going to blow my chance with you to go back to having bad sex with him, he had another thing coming."

I cleared my throat because I had to know. "Bad sex?"

"Fine," he conceded with a loud exhale. "Not bad, just not satisfying."

He thought I was scolding him. It was kind of sweet. As though I was trying to make him a better person by not letting him make blanket statements.

"You're right. I shouldn't just say something off-the-cuff. I need to back that up with empirical evidence," he added.

"No, you really don't."

"But sex shouldn't have rules about when and how long, like what days and what time. It should be more about spontaneity and wanting and being held down so you don't fly apart at the seams, right?" he asked expectantly.

"You sound like you think I'm going to argue with you."

He swallowed and then smiled, his eyes glistening with tears.

"What is this?" I asked, wiping his cheek with my thumb once he parked the car on the other side of the lot toward the beach. He'd driven us to a restaurant in Nahant called Tides. "Why're you crying?"

Big breath in. "I just—I'm scared that you're not going to give this a chance, and I don't want anything to mess things up because I just got you here."

"Oh no, don't worry about that," I said, hooking a hand behind his neck to ease him forward so I could give him a quick kiss. "After this is all over with your dad, I'm gonna date the hell out of you."

"You are?"

"I am."

"And when did you decide that?"

"Probably when I first saw you this afternoon," I admitted because, really, that was the truth. I'd taken one look at him and thought "home" for reasons that were completely illogical.

He sighed heavily. "That's a very romantic thing to say."

"Only you would think so."

"I have a request, though."

"Which is?"

"May I please have the sex part before everything gets figured out with my father?"

"We'll see if we can make time for that between the attempts on your life."

"That seems reasonable," he agreed before he lifted to kiss me.

I kissed him breathless, and he had trouble getting out of the car when I pulled back and ordered him to get moving.

"We could have sex right here," he offered as a nice family, parents and three little kids, walked by.

"That was classy," I chided. "Get in the restaurant."

"How about the bathroom once we get inside?"

It was damn flattering having such a pretty man bespelled, especially when I knew he was too good for me. But that didn't mean I was stupid enough to send him away. I would try to make him mine because he was right: two chance encounters was more than just luck. It was a sign. My whole life I'd gone with my gut, and I wasn't about to change that now.

I let Brin order because there were things he wanted me to try that he was excited about. We had a couple of beers, me the Sam Adams Nitro White, him the Newburyport Pale Ale, and fried calamari and cherry cola wings for starters and then more beer with our pizza. While he had a third, I stopped at two and went with water because I needed to be clearheaded to kill people, if necessary, and of course, now, drive.

His eggplant rollatini pizza looked a little odd but it tasted good, and my Meat Lover's hit the spot. It was noisy inside, just the kind of place I loved that was casual but had enough people that no one could sneak up behind me. The view of the beach was great too. When my phone rang, I felt like crap when I saw Doran's number because I'd forgotten to call Pravi back and that was probably what I was going to get yelled at about.

"Hey, sorry."

"No, is fine, is only your boss asking."

"Whatever, man," I groused. "But no package."

"You are sure?"

"Yeah, Doran, I'm sure. Brin said nothing came today."

"FedEx tracking shows it delivered."

So it wasn't just a casual question. "Well, I'll check around when we get back, see if it's on the porch or behind a plant or something, but he said he didn't get anything."

"You are positive."

"Yeah."

"Check again."

"Pardon me?"

"Look again for the package," he ordered.

I bristled instantly because where the hell did he get off ordering me around? Doran was a glorified chauffeur/bodyguard who'd never once been trusted to think on his own. He should never have presumed for a second that he could tell me to do anything. "Well, I can't right now because I'm at dinner."

"Why?"

"That's a dumbass question, don't you think?"

He coughed. "I mean why are you not in his home?"

"Because I wasn't worried about being out," I answered, wishing we were on the scrambled line because it was annoying to talk to him but not be able to speak plainly. I really wanted to tell him to go straight to hell.

"You need to go back."

"We will."

"Now."

I would have just hung up on him because he was being a dick and, more than that, I never, ever, took any order from Doran, but—something was off.

"What's going on?"

"Marko and I—we are looking for the package."

"Marko's with you?"

"Yes."

"Okay, so, this package, what's in it?"

He huffed out a breath, clearly irritated. "You need to return to the house, Ceaton."

"I will."

"That's not a request."

"It is to me," I said flippantly because, again, this was Doran trying to push me around. There was no way in hell that was going to fly.

Silence.

"We will see you soon."

I hung up as the waiter delivered a box for the leftover pizza. I'd scarfed down all of mine, but Brin had three slices of his left.

"You all right?"

I forced a smile. "Yeah, why?"

"You seem tense all of a sudden."

"Yeah, I am."

"I promise you nothing got delivered today that I saw."

"No, I know, you would have told me."

"Maybe they shoved it under the doormat," he suggested, draining the last of the bottle of Switchback Ale he'd finished the meal with.

"Well, we'll look when we get there, but I need you to listen to me for a second."

I had every drop of his focus.

"If I ever say run, you run—you understand?"

I had to make this very clear to him because I didn't trust Doran as far as I could throw him, and Grigor had separated Marko and me weeks ago, so God knew what he'd been filling Marko's head with. Not that I didn't trust Marko, because I did, but he was volatile in a way Pravi and Luka were not. In a pinch, would he back me or Doran? I hoped it would be me, always me, but I wasn't ready to bet my life on it.

"What?"

My focus returned sharply to Brin. "Just—any order I give you, you follow, you understand?"

"Of course."

I took his hand. "Even if you think I'm in trouble, if I tell you to—"

"Oh no," he said, dismissing me with an imperious wave.

"Pardon me?"

"Remember earlier when we were talking about Laine, and you were horrified that he left me to fend for myself with his ex?"

"This isn't the same thing."

"You're right, because I already have some pretty nice feelings for you, some warm and fuzzy, some hot and sweaty, but all good, so if you think I would ever run if you were in trouble, well then, you'd better think again."

I leaned back in my seat. "If that's how you really feel, then that means you won't listen to me if the shit hits that fan, and how the hell am I supposed to protect you?"

"Easily."

"And how's that?"

"You'll never leave me, and I'll be protected just fine."

"You're making light of something very serious," I warned.

"No, you're not listening to me," he corrected, standing up and sliding into the booth beside me, giving me no choice but to move over or have him in my lap. "I will do whatever you say, Ceaton Mercer, but I will never leave you."

I searched his face for any sign of give.

"You take care of your business, and I'll take care of you."

Grabbing his hand again, I pressed it over my heart. "You're killing me with this, but really, you have to follow directions when I give them to you."

He cupped my cheek. "Oh, baby, I will do anything you say, as long as you're right there with me."

"You're not hearing me."

"No," he said, smiling lazily as he brushed over my cheek with his thumb. "You're the one not listening. I'm sticking to you like glue. I'm not letting you get away a third time. What am I, stupid?"

"No, just stubborn."

Apparently, from the blinding smile I got, that was just fine with him.

I DROVE around the block to his house and circled once, checking, making sure there were no cars anywhere that Brin couldn't identify as belonging on the street. He cleared the Volvo S60, the Audi SUV, and the Toyota Camry parked along the curb.

"Just so you know," he said into the silence. "If we were walking, we could tell what cars belonged here and which ones didn't."

"How?" I wanted to know for future reference.

"One of the ways is that you have to have a sticker to park in the various beach parking lots," he educated me. "They cost around ten bucks a year, and everybody has one. I do, too, see?"

I saw where he was pointing and filed the information away.

"And that one too," he said, pointing at the bumper of the parked Audi.

I saw an oval about four inches across, like the OBX stickers for the Outer Banks in North Carolina that I'd seen before. On the Audi—and the Volvo, I noticed—there was an NHT one—for Nahant.

"I'll be sure to look out for these things," I assured him.

"Not that we'll be in this situation ever again."

"What's that?"

"Having to be so on guard."

He had no idea about the life he was in for.

"Not that I can't handle that, because I can do anything as long as we're together."

"You know you should really—"

"So what happens now?" he rushed out.

We were parked at the end of the street, and I was just looking, not ready to drive to the house quite yet.

"I'm considering things."

"What things?"

"Marko, mostly."

"Can you explain that a little?"

I checked the rearview mirror and both sides of the car before looking back at Brin's house. "Beyond this business with you and your father, I think my boss may possibly be ready to replace me."

"What does that mean?"

"It means that he could be worried that I have too much of my own power and not enough that doesn't flow through him."

"Okay, that makes sense."

"What?" I asked, turning to look at him.

"What?" He shrugged. "If I'm a crime boss, I don't want the people under me to get the idea that the guy between them and me is more qualified than me. I mean, I want him—in this case you—to always be subordinate to me, and I want them to see you're not qualified to do my job."

"Right. Yes."

"And at the moment, it sounds like Grigor is worried that you're going to push him out."

"Which is ridiculous because a non-Serbian guy cannot run the Serbian mob in Boston," I said incredulously. "If he thought about it for even a second, he'd get how stupid it is."

"Not to mention the fact that you're made loyal."

"Yes, I am." I sighed, reaching over to pat his knee. "And it says something about Grigor that after all this time he doesn't get that, but you do after knowing me for only an afternoon."

He covered my hand with his, and only then did I realize he was practically bouncing in his seat.

"What's goin' on with you?"

"This is so exhilarating," he announced excitedly.

I glanced over at him.

"What? Is it time to run?"

"This is not a movie," I insisted.

"Yes, I know," he marveled. "This is my life at the moment."

He was much too hopped up on adrenaline and alcohol to be clearheaded.

I parked the Beetle in his garage, and the door was closing as I heard a car stop on the other side.

"Get out." I barked the order at Brin.

Moving fast, he scrambled out of his seat with the leftovers in hand and then stood there waiting for whatever I was going to say next. It was amusing, the frantic eagerness on his face as he clutched the rest of his pizza.

"You might have to run for your life," I told him. "You maybe wanna ditch that."

He tipped his head back and forth, clearly on the fence about that. "But it's really great pizza, and I have a good feeling about the outcome of all this, and I'd hate to have tossed it for nothing."

"A good feeling?"

He nodded.

"You realize we might both die here."

"Not today. I just got you; I'm not ready for it to be over."

"You don't have me," I argued even as I realized how ridiculous I sounded. I really needed to focus.

"Oh, the hell I don't. You're all mine."

I threw up my hands, pulled my gun, and told him to stay right behind me.

"Yes, dear."

This was serious and he had me smiling, and that was bad because our situation was in fact, perilous, but his words, all of them, from now to back when I first walked through his door, made me so happy.

And I knew why: they signaled hope.

Having grown up without anyone, no family, and then in and out of foster care until I was old enough to join the Marines… Brinley and his words of promise signaled a deep and resonating longing. I was convinced that people who never had the warmth and nurturing of a home knew instinctively when it was being offered. When shelter and commitment and forever were on the table, it was instantly recognizable and not something to be taken lightly or for granted. I would do neither.

"You're playing with fire," I told him as we crept closer to the door.

"Oh?"

"You better not take anything you've said back after the excitement wears off."

"I would never," he assured me. "I'm keeping you."

"We should talk about—"

"May I ask a question?"

"Now?"

"Yeah."

"Brin, you—"

"Does this kind of thing happen to you a lot?"

"What?"

"People trying to kill you?"

"Yes and no. It's not usually me specifically," I explained. "It's us—Grigor and the rest of the crew collectively—that other people try to kill."

"Ah. So that's a yes, then."

I turned and looked at Brin. "Yeah, this kind of thing happens to me fairly regular."

"Okay."

"Okay?"

"Yeah, it's okay. As long as I know what I'm in for, I'll be prepared."

"For what?"

"To be a gangster's moll."

"I'm sorry, *what* did you just say?"

"I thought you needed to focus. You were all worried about me carrying my food."

I shook my head. "Just—be ready to run, all right?"

"As long as you come with me."

He was driving me nuts.

Putting a finger to my mouth, I leaned into the kitchen and a bullet hit the doorframe beside me.

So stupid.

I rushed into the room and saw Luka moving out of the corner of my left eye, but I knew Doran, who was on my right, had been the one who fired based on the trajectory of the shot. So I fired there first, twice, then dropped into a crouch to duck the return fire and waited.

"What are you doing?" Luka called over to me.

"I'm waiting to see if you're going to shoot at me."

"Why the fuck would I shoot at you?" he asked irritably.

"I dunno! But nothing makes sense today."

"Well, you and I do. Always."

Letting out a deep breath, I rose, checked around fast, saw no one else, and then walked over first to Doran, who was dead, one bullet in his forehead, the other in his throat, and then moved over to Luka, who was lying on the floor clutching his left shoulder.

"What's wrong, you hurt yourself playing racquetball or something?" I asked, holstering my gun before squatting down beside him.

"No," he grumbled, struggling to sit up until I helped him. "When Doran fell, he fired and hit me."

"Are you serious?"

"Yes," he rasped, moving the shawl collar of the camel hair topcoat so I could see the slowly seeping blood. "This is brand new and it's ruined."

"What the fuck are you doing here with Doran anyway?" I asked, pulling a dishtowel from the handle of the stove and passing it to him.

"What am I doing with this?"

I growled before manhandling him, getting into his coat and then underneath, to his suit jacket and finally to the turtleneck cashmere sweater. Once I lifted that, I took a quick second to fold the towel and then shove it over the gunshot wound.

"You could have just said," he griped at me.

"The hell are you doing with Doran?" I railed at him, furious that he could have actually been hurt, or even killed, because of an accident.

"I'm not *with* Doran; Marko was with Doran."

"Then what the hell are you doing here?"

"I came to make sure you were all right."

"For fuck's sake, Luka, you could've been killed!"

"You could have too, that was the fuckin' point."

I had no idea what to say. It warmed my heart to know that my friend had made a trip specifically to save my life, should I have needed his assistance. On the other hand, he'd just made it crystal clear to our boss where his loyalty lay. If Grigor was, in fact, gunning for me, Luka would be dead right after me.

"You're an idiot," was all I could think of to say.

"Yes, well, I love you too."

I groaned, rubbed the bridge of my nose too hard, and then looked back up at the man now smiling at me.

"Where the hell did you park?"

"On the next street over. I didn't want Doran to see me."

What he was saying registered. "So you actually did come to save me from Doran."

"No, I came to save you from Marko, if that was how it went down."

I nodded. "Yeah, I dunno whose side Marko's gonna be on, either."

"It could go either way," Luka told me as I helped him to his feet. "Maybe."

"What're you talking about?"

"Marko," he replied simply. "Some days I think he loves you like a brother, might even like me too. Other days, I think he wants to put a bullet in both of us."

I felt the same. It was dicey with Marko. But as Luka said, maybe. The thing was, there was every possibility that we'd all been reading the scary man wrong. He might have loved all of us—me, Luka, and Pravi—something fierce. There was just no way of locking it down.

"Okay, so now what?" Luka wanted to know.

"You tell me. Is Grigor trying to kill me because he thinks I'm trying to make a move on him or for some other reason?"

"At the moment, some other reason."

"And what is that?"

"Judge Hardin is dead."

"Oh," Brin sighed behind me, moving up slowly, carrying a large envelope. "That's too bad. He was still so young."

"Where was that?" I asked him.

"In the garage," he told me. "I remembered that a lot of delivery guys slip things under the garage door if I'm not home."

There were tire marks on it. "So we ran over it when we came in?" He nodded.

I looked back to Luka. "Did Grigor kill the judge?"

But he was looking past me at Brin. "Hey, I know you."

Oh, for fuck's sake.

"I think we got drunk together on the Fourth of July."

"You *were* really drunk," Brin assured him.

"Yeah, I was," Luka agreed. "You were asking a lot of questions about Ceaton."

"Which you didn't answer," Brin acknowledged, "but you were very kind to explain all about my father and his dealings with your boss."

Luka turned to me. "Don't tell Grigor, okay?"

"Why the fuck would I tell Grigor?"

"Yeah, I guess."

"Luka!"

"What, Jesus."

"Did Grigor kill the judge?"

"Well, yeah."

Brin caught his breath. "Ohmygod, I thought when you said he died that he had a heart attack or something."

I squinted at him, and I was sure Luka must have been looking at him with a similar expression of disbelief because he recoiled from both of us.

"What?"

Luka made a noise of disgust, returning my focus to him. "Listen, Grigor killed the judge because he was going to come clean about his criminal activities. Apparently the FBI had him on bribery, racketeering—you name it, they had it. But one of the girls the judge has been sleeping with got news to him, and he put his journal with all the dates and times and amounts in it in an envelope and sent it here to his kid for safekeeping."

"Why not just give it to the Feds?"

"He wanted to make a deal with them, and he knew when they tossed his place that they'd find everything. He had some clerk in his office take care of sending it out."

"How did Grigor get to the judge?"

"He had Graham do it."

I was stunned. "Jonas Graham?"

He nodded.

"The lawyer," I said flatly.

"Yeah."

"He sent a lawyer to kill a judge."

"He did. He told Graham that it was time to earn his keep because there was no way in hell the judge was letting anyone else into his home."

That did make sense.

"Like Marko couldn't have gotten in there, or me or Pravi, after the judge locked everything down tight."

True. Someone would have at least noticed a ruckus.

"Or even you. The judge was a smart man."

I wasn't inclined to agree. He'd turned his back on a woman who loved him and the best son a father could ask for—in my opinion—to retain his money and status. Smart wasn't something I equated with the man.

"So what happened?"

"You're going to love this," he sighed. "The judge killed Graham."

"No shit?"

"Yeah. When Graham pushed the judge off the balcony of his penthouse, he took him with him. That was like, ten minutes ago."

I turned to look at Brin. "I'm so sorry, baby."

He shook his head. "I don't really care. I just need to know what this means for you."

Turning back to Luka, I checked the gunshot and saw it was no longer bleeding. "Can you drive yourself to the hospital or not?"

"Why? If I can't, are you going to take me?"

"You know I will."

He rolled his eyes. "I'll go to the hospital, say I got shot in a drive-by wherever, and stay there until they let me out."

"Tell your mother it wasn't me."

"Yeah, yeah."

I thought of something. "Why the hell did Grigor send me out here to begin with if he was just gonna have you guys kill me?"

"He wasn't planning on killing you," Luka said as I walked beside him to the front door. "He decided when you told Pravi that you couldn't find the package."

I nodded. "He thought I was holding out on him."

"Yeah."

"So years of loyalty count for shit," I groused.

"Please," he said with exaggerated patience. "Grigor's insane. For him to think that you, of all of us, would ever turn on him, shows me how paranoid he's become."

"I thought it was a family. I thought we were a family."

"I would say they were wolves, but wolves wouldn't turn on each other like that."

"Yeah," I agreed. "So I'll call Grigor, tell him I shot you."

"No, no, no," Luka said, turning to me. "I'll call Grigor, because if I do it and tell him what happened, then maybe he lets you live."

"For what?" I prodded. "You know as well as I do. Once he decides to kill you, it's gonna get done eventually. I'm not one of his men anymore; it happened that fast just because he thought something that was totally bullshit."

"He trusted you this morning when he woke up."

"I'm not so sure about that. He's been having second thoughts about me for a while now," I said sadly, more hurt than I thought I was, and now with a slow, seething rage eating into my gut because Brin was involved as well. Brin was in just as much danger as I was because if Grigor was gunning for me, Brin was in his sights too.

"Yeah, but he wasn't planning to put a bullet in you, so I still think he could be persuaded to change his mind."

"No. It's done," I said, choking on the finality of it and the stand that I had to make. And how terrifyingly alone I felt. How was I supposed to keep Brin alive if Grigor came after me with all his men and all his resources? I was one, he was many, and it was just a matter of time before I was swallowed by that ocean.

Luka cleared his throat. "If you call him, he might come himself. I don't want that because he'll make a knee-jerk decision. He needs to remember what you mean to him."

I sighed deeply.

"You could run."

I shook my head. "I can't. Brin's life is here."

He shrugged. "Give him the book, swear loyalty, do whatever you have to, just…. You can still walk away from this in one piece. I would miss you if you were dead."

"Thank you, buddy," I said gently, squeezing his good shoulder. "Now, if I put Doran in the trunk, can you dump the car off with Otto and still get to the hospital?"

"Yeah, sure. You did me a favor and didn't kill me, plus you gave me a nice excuse to give Grigor. I can drop off the body, no problem."

"Are you sure you can do that?" Brin asked. "You lost a lot of blood."

"It's only a shoulder wound," Luka explained. "I'll live."

Brin gave him a wan smile.

"I'll call him as soon as you leave."

"What did I just say?" Luka shouted.

"It doesn't matter. Use your head."

He stared at me.

"Think," I ordered. "What's the only real alternative here?"

"Okay," Luka agreed and went out the door first because I had to pick up now-lifeless Doran, a guy I'd drank with just the night before.

It was surreal.

I'd always heard that in the mob, if you lost your boss, life could change in the blink of an eye. I was naïve to think the same would not be true if your boss got it in his head that you were disloyal. It was a shame. I'd thought to spend the rest of my life working for Grigor Jankovic, and now, if I saw him again, he'd try to kill me.

After I put Doran in the trunk of one of Grigor's many cars, this one his new Mercedes S-Class Sedan, I walked around to the driver's side and clasped Luka's outstretched hand.

"I'm going to go to the hospital and call my mother and then wait to hear from you."

"I probably won't make it out of here."

"Nah, I don't accept that. I'll wait for you to call."

"Luka, I—"

"I'll wait."

I shook my head even as he held on to my hand tighter.

"In there you said 'I thought we were a family,' but you need to understand that we *are* a family. It just doesn't include Grigor."

Jesus. He was looking at me with the same hopefulness that Brin did, and it was gutting me because I wasn't sure if I could live up to it. I really didn't want to die and let him down.

"Be careful," I ordered. "And take care of your mother."

"I will," he groaned, wincing as he moved his shoulder. "She's gonna be pissed."

"Just make sure she knows it wasn't me who shot you."

He gave me a smile, and I stood there and watched him drive away.

Back inside I found Brin cleaning up his kitchen.

"Let me do that," I told him.

He looked up at me from where he was kneeling on the floor. "It's blood, Ceaton; I've seen a lot of it in my life. People get hurt out on boats and around the water. I've seen people die, animals.... I had to look for a colleague's severed foot once."

"Holy shit."

"I'm not some ingénue who's going to faint at the sight of blood."

"Okay."

"You know those shows where you watch those guys out on the fishing boats who catch crab or tuna?"

"Yeah."

"I've been on those boats, and it's way worse than what you see."

I walked over and took hold of his arm, lifting him up off his knees. "So you're telling me you're hardcore, then."

"Yes."

I nodded and took his face in my hands. "Does it bother you to have me touch you?"

"No," he said, trembling, "why would it?"

"Because I just shot a man to death in your kitchen," I reminded him.

"He would have killed you," he said, lifting his head so my hands fell away and then stepped in to me, wrapping his arms around my waist. "And then he would have killed me. He didn't even give you time to explain; he just came here to end your life."

"I know," I said, clutching him tight, resting my face in his soft, clean-smelling hair.

"I'm not freaked out because you killed him—again, scientist. I know about life and death. I'm scared that you could be hurt or killed, and that's what has me sort of frantic."

"How do you mean?"

"I think we should run," he said nervously, leaning back to look into my face. "I think I should pack a bag and we should drive to Canada or something."

"Should we?"

"It's a lovely country and their Prime Minister is really hot."

I chuckled.

"It's not funny. How are you so calm?"

"Because we have to be smart about this, and I refuse to take you away from your life."

"What does that mean?"

"That means we're going to call the police and they'll put you in protective custody, and if you turn over the book, then—"

"What? Witness protection? And I never see you or my folks again?"

"At least you'll be alive."

"Didn't you just explain to your friend about how you weren't going to take me away from my life?"

"That was before I actually thought about you dead at my feet."

"Well, I don't care. I don't want to be alive if I can't have you with me and I never see my parents again or any of my friends or extended family. What kind of life is that?"

"Honey—"

"Oh, don't get all sweet and lovey-dovey now," he warned. "I told you before and I'll tell you again—I am not leaving you, no way, no how."

"It's different than it was. You—"

"The hell it is," he countered. "What I want has not changed an iota."

"Brin—"

"No." He was adamant. "You should call your boss, find out what he's planning, and open that envelope while you're at it."

I didn't have time to argue with him. Pulling out my phone, I scrolled to Grigor and pushed the button while I opened the package Judge Hardin had sent to Brin.

"Ceaton," Grigor answered. "I'm really not surprised to hear from you."

"I hope, for both our sakes, that I'm getting you on a secure line."

"You are."

"That's good, because I'm telling you now, I put a bullet in Luka and Doran's dead."

He sighed. "Why didn't you kill Luka?"

"I needed someone to take the body."

"You've always been very pragmatic."

"'Thorough' is the word you're looking for."

"And will Luka live?"

"I think so, but he lost a lot of blood," I lied.

"Did Doran suffer?"

"Do you care?"

"I do."

"No. He didn't suffer," I said, looking outside and noting it was dark already. The days were so short in the fall. "So tell me, who're you gonna send to finish me off?"

"I'm going to send everyone, Ceaton."

"Even Marko, your top guy?"

"You're my top guy, Ceaton. Always have been."

"Oh?"

"You know that."

"I didn't."

"I've never trusted anyone as I did you."

Did. Past tense already. "Then I don't get it."

His exhale was long. "When Brinley asked for you specifically and you didn't do more to get out of going, I knew something was amiss."

Ah.

"And then when the judge confessed to Graham that he'd sent his son his ledger, I knew what you were up to."

"Did you."

"Of course. I'm not a fool."

But he was.

"You were making a play to take over," he announced. "You've been planning it for a while, and this was the final piece you needed. You even tried to talk Jonas into corroborating with you. I saw your number on his phone earlier today."

Poor guy; he only wanted to get laid. "Is that why you sent him to kill the judge? Was it a test to see if he'd do it?"

"Of course," Grigor told me. "Anyone on your side, anyone trying to put you in my place, was dealt with today."

"And now what? You and Pravi are on your way out here to Nahant to finish off me and Brin?"

"It's Brin now?"

"Yeah."

"First tell me the real reason you let Luka live."

Oh no. "Because he came with Doran, and Doran was the better shot."

"I see."

"Luka's not with me."

"And Pravi?"

"Pravi? Are you kidding? He's been with you the longest."

"And yet when I told him to take some men and go out there and kill you, he left without saying good-bye, and I haven't seen him since."

"That doesn't mean anything."

"I think it means everything."

Shit. "So now what?"

"Do you have the book?"

"I do."

"Well, then, perhaps we can make a trade."

It was bullshit, I knew better. Grigor Jankovic never made deals with anyone, especially not when he had the upper hand as he certainly did now. "Like what?" I played along. "Me, Brin, Luka, and Pravi for the book?"

"They *are* with you, then."

"Yeah, sure," I said, texting Luka, telling him to ditch the car anywhere and just go to the hospital and call his mother. He needed to make sure she was safe too. "So about that trade."

"There's no trade, Ceaton! That book is useless. The clerk worked for me. She sent Brinley an empty journal."

But as I got the package open, I found a sort of squashed diary with one of those locks that had a key. It was a little girl's diary, pink and mauve with a ballerina on the cover. The most important thing, though, was what it said on the outside.

"What is this?" I murmured.

"What is what?"

"I opened the package and there's a diary in here, but it says the original is with the vault," I husked, bewildered. What I was looking at?

"I'm sorry?"

I snapped a picture of it with my phone and texted it to him. "The fuck is the vault, and shouldn't this say that the original is *in* the vault, not *with*?"

There was a long silence.

"Grigor?"

"Who—how do you know the vault, Ceaton?"

"I have no idea what you're talking about."

"Everyone is already on their way and you're dead, and so is Pravi and Luka and anyone else I find!" he rasped, sounding almost hysterical, unhinged like I'd never heard him before. He was out of his mind, and what the hell was the vault? "I hope you enjoy watching Brin die in front of you!"

"Fuck you!" I roared before I hung up.

"Ceaton?" Brin asked as he washed his hands and turned to me. "What's wrong?"

"We've gotta get out of here, back to my place to get my guns and—"

We both heard the cars screaming to a halt in front of the house.

"Fuck," I shouted, rushing to the front door, knowing I hadn't locked it after I came in from walking Luka out.

It flew open and Pravi leaped inside, landing almost at my feet with Marko right behind him.

"Down!" Marko yelled, and I dropped to my knees as the air was filled with bullets that tore into the wall on the opposite side of the room.

Scrambling to the door, I slammed it shut, got up, and locked it before crawling back to Pravi. "The fuck are you doing here?"

"I came to warn you," he snarled, clearly not happy with the position he found himself in. "Grigor's lost his fucking mind, and you're his scapegoat."

I turned to Marko, who was now sitting beside him, jaw clenched, utterly furious. "And you?"

"I came to keep both of you safe from Grigor!"

"Why're you yelling?"

"Because this is your fault," he snarled.

"Why is this my fault?"

"Because we," Marko said, indicating Pravi, me, and himself, "should have killed Grigor months ago when I first told you that he wanted to kill you."

I couldn't help smiling at him.

"Now you too are insane?"

"No, I'm just—" I sucked in a breath as my vision blurred around the edges. "I figured Pravi would come, but you—"

"You thought I would leave you to the wolves?"

"It took a lot of faith, yanno?"

His scoff was loud. "I have you, I have Pravi, maybe Luka, is hard to tell, but that is all. If I am done, I will lie down with my brothers."

"Fuck," I groaned as the tears filled my eyes.

"Could we not do this right fucking now!" Pravi shouted. "I'm not ready to die yet!"

Bullets strafed the windows, and Brin crawled over to me even though I ordered him to stay safely down behind the counters in the kitchen.

"I belong with you," he announced, bumping up beside me, huddling close.

"Oh, that's so sweet," Pravi quipped, casting me a long-suffering look.

"Why would you come to warn me?" I asked, looking at him. "You're Grigor's guy."

"You know I'm your guy first, don't be stupid," he assured me, hands covering his head as the four of us were showered with glass and wood. There was only so much protection we could have.

"It's like seven at night on a Sunday," I gasped, looking at Brin. "How are people not calling the cops?"

"Suppressors on guns," Marko offered by way of explanation, "and they are close to the house, and there is only beach and a park on other side of this street."

I stared at him.

"And wind," he rambled, "is very noisy."

"You about done?"

"What?"

"Did you happen to bring any more guns or ammo?"

"I came from Grigor to here; I did not stop and do any shopping on the way."

I had no idea he could be so sarcastic. I'd totally missed that in years of apparent friendship.

I glanced back at Pravi.

"I didn't hit Walmart either," he remarked dryly.

They were both assholes, but they were most definitely *my* assholes since they were willing to die for me.

I sent Marko into the kitchen, then Pravi, then Brin, and I followed. We headed to the garage, and I stood in the doorway as Pravi crouched and Marko stood behind me, all of us putting the suppressors on our guns as well. I had an extra mag and knew both of them did as well—we all always carried one—but that was it, and I knew Grigor had a lot of guys.

"How many cars are out there?" I asked Marko.

"Five, I think."

I coughed. "After we're done here, we've gotta go make sure Luka is safe too."

"And his mother," Pravi added.

"Yeah."

We all listened hard, not talking.

"I am lucky," Marko said into the silence. "I am orphan like you, so nobody else to worry for."

"Excuse me," Brin chimed in from behind him. "He has me."

"I have him," I agreed, reaching back to take his hand and give it a squeeze.

"If we live through this, I will dance at your wedding," Marko promised.

"Wedding?" I blurted.

"Awesome," Brin said cheerfully.

"Focus," I demanded.

"You are not the boss," Pravi growled, taking a moment to point an accusatory finger at me. "Remember that."

It was quiet again, and after a few minutes, the constant readiness took its toll.

"I killed Anton Djordjevic," Marko said into the silence.

Despite the depth of shit we were in, I couldn't help turning to look at him, and neither could Pravi.

"The hell you say," I gasped.

He grunted.

"Marko, what the fuck?" Pravi sounded just as stunned as I did.

"You know he ordered Aristov to kill Pavle, Goran, and Sava. Everyone knew. He thought because he had McNamara he was safe. I showed him he was not."

I must have looked like an idiot with my mouth open and no sound coming out.

"He was coming for Grigor; they have been circling each other like mongoose and cobra. The end was coming."

"But it's all the same mob in Belgrade," I reminded him, my voice rising in fear for my friend. "And when Grigor finds out that you—"

"He knows. I took photo."

"Oh, for crissakes, Marko, you—"

"Yes, yes," he grumbled, waving me off. "It is all done and now men in Belgrade will want to know why Grigor ordered the hit."

"Oh shit," I breathed out.

"Did you kill McNamara too?" Pravi questioned.

"He was there; you know I hate mess."

My sigh was long. "You know you just put Grigor in deep shit."

He shrugged. "My gift to him. Both men were trash."

No argument. One of the many ways Anton Djordjevic had distinguished his business from Grigor's was by embracing the sex trade. He'd had several brothels and men and women out on the street actively recruiting young girls. Pravi and I had spent one of our few and far between days off just walking the streets around the bus stations, handing out cash to the lost waifs we saw before Djordjevic's people pounced on them. It was no contest between us and them because I had Pravi with me. The little girls took one look at him and flocked. No one else stood a chance.

"Yes?"

"Yes," I agreed with Marko.

"So they are dead and Grigor must answer. I say, is good day."

His sense of morality may have been skewed, but so was mine. And without a doubt, there were people who would have a chance at a new life because of Marko's actions.

"You know if we weren't dead before, we are now?"

Marko grimaced.

"I didn't do anything," Pravi was quick to point out.

"You're here with me, aren't you?"

"Yeah," he whined, long-suffering as always.

"And you think *I* need to focus?" Brin said, smirking at me. "Wow."

I would have answered him, but the front door banged open and I heard a lot of boots on the hardwood floor. No one came around the corner though, instead remaining on the other side of the kitchen wall.

"Pravi!" Aca yelled. "I talked to Grigor, and he said that if you shoot Ceaton, he'll forgive you, so do it now!"

Pravi tipped his head to look up at me, and I looked down. "Aca?" He mouthed the name at me.

"Blood," I mouthed back, and we both knew what I meant.

At a time like this, of upheaval, when you weren't sure who to trust, those related to you by blood were everything. Grigor had turned to the only guy he knew he could trust implicitly. It was the smart play, or would have been, if Aca wasn't such an idiot.

"Pravi!" Aca yelled again. "Ceaton's the one we want!"

If I thought for a second that Grigor would actually let Brin, and Pravi and Marko, and even Luka live if I surrendered myself… I would. But my boss had already proven today he had no honor, so I said nothing as Pravi told Aca to go to hell.

"Marko," he called out like he was an afterthought.

"Fuck you!" Marko roared back, which wasn't a surprise. "I know he wants me dead! I am not idiot, no matter what your boss thinks!"

"You're all dead men!"

Quite possibly.

I turned to look at Brin. "Whatever happens, stay right beside me."

He nodded, and I saw it in his eyes, the faith and trust there. I really wanted to live so I could prove him right about me.

"I—"

"I know, baby," he soothed me, hand lifting to my face for just a moment, his touch featherlight and so comforting.

"Pra—"

Pop. And then another and another, and I knew the sound of gunshots, but nothing came at us, no bullets hit the wall or the refrigerator or the stove. There was no one visible through the window out of the kitchen and nothing hit the garage door.

I stayed still, so did Pravi, so did Marko. And then there was a knocking on the wall.

"Ceaton Mercer?"

Different voice, deeper, resonate, not Aca at all… but a voice that sounded vaguely familiar.

"Yes?"

"Don't shoot, and don't let your men shoot either."

"You're not the boss," Pravi reiterated, but he didn't yell it out.

I flicked him on the back of the neck to shut him up. "Okay," I called back.

Then a hand holding a Beretta 92FS without a suppressor— whoever he was, he clearly wasn't worried about making noise—and then a head tipped out from behind the wall.

I had that instant jolt of recognition like I'd seen him somewhere important, like I should have known who he was, but didn't. I knew his face, but his name escaped me.

"Ceaton Mercer," he greeted me.

"Yeah," I answered as Brin leaned around me, putting a hand on Pravi's shoulder to see who I was talking to. "Who are you?"

"You don't know?"

But I did, didn't I? I just had to dredge up the name.

"Could you get back behind me," I ordered Brin without moving my gaze from the man now in the middle of his kitchen.

"Who are you?" Brin asked, taking in the predatory ease of the man before us. Even with all the guns pointed at him—mine, Marko's, and Pravi's—he wasn't nervous in the least.

Slowly, carefully, he holstered the Beretta, keeping his gaze fixed on Brin the whole time. "I'm Darius Hawthorne," he explained. "And I go by a lot of names, but that's the one he should know," he said, pointing at me.

I cleared my throat. "What other names do you go by?" I asked, because that one was not ringing any bells.

"Conrad Harris," he answered, his voice with a quality about it that was instantly soothing, "and Terrence Moss, and the one you'll for sure remember is Gold Team Leader."

It was like he zapped me with a Taser.

My knees almost buckled, and I had to grab for the wall but got Marko instead. It was lucky he was so big, so strong, because I yanked on his arm as I fought for balance.

I was overcome, undone, lightheaded and almost nauseated; at the same time it felt like my skin was too tight as my eyes filled for the second time that night.

I took quick, shallow breaths so I wouldn't pass out as my face heated, and I shivered in the cold air I hadn't noticed a moment ago.

No doubt about it, I was having the weirdest day *ever*.

"Mercer?"

"Holy fucking shit."

His smile spread slowly and was infinitely kind and just a bit wicked. Gorgeous man, but even more importantly, scary with a confidence you could feel charging the air with electricity.

"Sir," I said, my military training back in an instant. I almost saluted.

He crossed the room then, hand out, coming fast, and I pushed away from Marko, scrambled around Pravi, and rushed to meet him.

I clasped the offered hand tight, and he covered it with his other.

"I—so you know, I would never—I didn't—I couldn't—I'm not the kind of man who would have ever left you or the others, and—I swear to you I did *not*," I vowed, wanting him to hear me, needing him to hear me, overwhelmed with the opportunity I had in the middle of the most fucked-up and amazing day I could ever remember having.

There had been good days and there had been soul-sucking bad ones, but never one that was all those things rolled up together.

It had started out so normally, so nondescript in every way, and yet now I was inextricably changed. Forever.

When the day began, there was no Brin, but now there was the promise of him and where we could go together and what we could possibly become.

I was always friendly with Luka but had never thought of him as ready to put his life on the line for me. Now, though, I knew better. Knew he saw us as close and that he would share the weight of our friendship and whatever that brought him.

Pravi was always the one I counted on to have my back, but I hadn't known he considered us more, closer, brothers even, willing to stand with me, beside me, and in front of me if needed.

And Marko—Jesus—he'd been the biggest surprise because he was the wild card, the one I had never been able to pin down to know, beyond a shadow of a doubt, that he was altogether and inextricably mine. It was like I had no idea who I had in my life until there was the possibility I could lose them.

But now… I had the opportunity I never hoped to have. I could explain to the man the Army had lied to that I did *not*, in fact, abandon my position and then decide to leave him and the others dangling in the wind without protection in the middle of a firefight. I wasn't made that way, and now I could tell him.

"Sir, I didn't abandon you or the others when—"

He squeezed my hand tight, stopping me as I searched his face. "I know," he assured me. "I always knew. That's why I'm here. My circumstances have changed, and I find myself in need of a full-time, permanent team, and I need someone to lead them. I was hoping I could convince you to take the job."

Surreal. My day was officially nuts. I had no idea what the hell was going on.

"Mercer?"

"I… am about to quite possibly be dead, sir, and I have no idea how you're even here at the moment, let alone here, period, but it's doubtful if you—with just the skill set I know about—are in any way in need of a team leader."

He put his free hand on my shoulder but didn't release the other. "Here's the thing," he said, smiling at me. "You're right: leader isn't it. Backup is. I need someone to have my back at all times."

"What is it that you do, sir, because I really only have one set of skills."

"Which is precisely why I came to find you."

CHAPTER EIGHT

THE DAY I had thought could get no stranger just had.

Sitting with Brin on my right and Pravi and Marko on my left as I faced a man I had only ever seen once before… was overwhelming. The fact that we were doing it in Darius's house in Nahant—well, a house he was thinking about buying and therefore trying out at the moment—was even more odd. In the warm and sumptuously decorated living room with a bay window that looked out at the sea, I was almost as comfortable as I'd been earlier in the day at Brin's house.

Almost.

"So," Darius began, leaning forward, speaking to Brin, "you can stay here until your house is put back in order—bullets out of the walls, blood off the floor—that kind of thing. I'm leaving on business to collect resources, so this house is yours in the meantime."

"Thank you," Brin replied kindly, as enraptured as the rest of us with Darius.

"I'm sorry I didn't get here earlier. We could have skipped the scene where your home was caught in a hail of gunfire."

"Would you mind starting at the beginning?" Brin asked. "Some of us are playing catch-up here."

Darius chuckled, leaning back on the black leather couch, clearly charmed. "Where would you like me to start?"

"I think just a general overview would work."

He thought a second. "All right, well, I used to kill people. A lot of people. You could hire me, and I would make whoever you needed to disappear, disappear. Or if you wanted something to be public and messy, I could do that too. I also worked for an arm of the CIA that basically sent me to a place, and if I succeeded, great, and if I didn't, then they would leave me to rot and I'd end up being some dead guy that nobody ever heard of."

"That's horrible," Brin gasped.

"That's Black Ops," Darius said implacably. "And it's the life."

Now looking him over, I realized I'd never really seen him before. Our one and only meeting had been brief, and my memory involved a helmet and a mere glimpse of the sea green of his eyes. The man sitting before me now with a goatee and a fade haircut, massive shoulders, wide chest, long legs—all of him powerful and muscular but not bulky, sleek, with a coiled readiness, as though he was deciding whether to kill us— this was all brand new. His eyes were a brighter jade than I remembered, and the sharp contrast to his tawny umber skin with the golden-bronze undertones was striking. As he sat now in front of me, I had so many questions it was difficult to know where to start.

"What does any of this have to do with me?" was all I could come up with.

He cleared his throat and leaned forward.

"May I ask something first?" Pravi interrupted.

Darius glanced at me. "Is that all right?"

"Yes, of course," I almost sputtered, amazed I was even being consulted.

"Go ahead," he told Pravi.

"What happened to all Grigor's men?"

"The fifteen that were outside?" Darius clarified. "Is that who you mean?"

"Yeah."

"They're gone," he said without a sliver of emotion before giving Brin a new smile that made his eyes gleam dangerously. "And I have people taking care of the mess to make sure that none of your neighbors are alerted. I don't want you to get a violent reputation."

I was surprised by Brin's snort of laughter, but at the same time, not. He took things in stride, my boy; I'd already found that out earlier.

"Will Grigor come after us?" Marko inquired, though his voice sounded gravelly and low. He wasn't scared, never scared, but he was cautious. "I had busy day."

"Yes, you did," Darius agreed with a rakish grin. "But Grigor, like many, has heard about the vault, and because he knows that the judge's diary has been acquired by me—no, he won't bother you again."

"And his link to the judge?" I asked him.

"He'll have to answer for what the lawyer, Graham, was doing there, but that's not your problem anymore. As of this moment, neither you, Pravi, Marko, nor Luka work with, or for, Grigor Jankovic."

I was quiet. So were the others, waiting.

"You work for me," Darius said, his gaze meeting mine, "and Pravi and Marko and Luka are your men."

Pravi opened his mouth to dispute the moniker, but I put my hand on his knee to keep him quiet.

"So if I'm getting this right," I began slowly, "you were a CIA assassin and also a freelance contract killer, but now, suddenly, you find yourself with a new position that has you 'acquiring items,' and because of that, you need backup."

"Excellent summary," he agreed.

"May I ask what prompted you to want to change?"

"I have a friend who needed me to watch over him, and so I had to be less on the go and more able to monitor him."

"You were protecting him."

"Yes."

"And does he still need protection?"

"For a bit longer, yes."

"And when he doesn't, will you go back to the CIA and your freelance work?"

"It doesn't work like that," Darius explained patiently. "Being the vault is a position you keep until you're ready to retire… or someone retires you first."

"May I ask another question?"

"As many as you like."

"Why me?"

Darius leaned forward and met my gaze. "You didn't leave me and my team; you protected us and had our back until you and your partner were blown up and he was killed."

"Yes."

"You're one of the best marksmen I've ever seen, you're calm under pressure, you think before you act, you have excellent instincts, quick reflexes, and above all, you're loyal."

"I—"

"The brass blamed you because you *didn't* leave and your partner died. Your lieutenant ordered your unit out of the firefight, but you disregarded orders and remained behind to make sure that my men and I had a clear escape route. I knew exactly who ran and who stayed. I'm sorry I couldn't do anything about it, but we were never there."

I sucked in a breath, swallowed hard, willed myself to not break down or scream. It wasn't fair. I'd done the right thing, the ethical thing, the moral thing, and I'd lost my future because of it. I'd had a plan that was washed away in a single moment. I remembered how the others looked at me after, what I was called and known for. They said I was insubordinate, that I deserted my team, my post, men who were supposed to be my family, and worst of all, got my partner killed.

I'd known better, known the truth, but it was cold comfort day after day. As Tanner's father had said to me when I went to see him and his wife once I was stateside, he wished that I'd gotten the chance to prove them all wrong. Instead, I was simply done, simply gone.

But now, this man was telling me he knew the truth, knew who I was, how I was made. I had no words that would ever be enough.

"I understand that Tanner received a Purple Heart."

"He deserved it."

"You deserved to be honored as well."

"I just wanted you to know, sir."

"I most certainly did and once the Army and I parted ways," he continued, "before I was asked to be a contractor for the company, I made it a point to find you. I'm sorry I wasn't able to contact you right away, but that could have been dangerous for you."

I was in the *mob*. I had to wonder how much more scary his life had to have been in the past few years to think mine was safe.

"I have very few friends, Mercer—I'd like you to be one."

I cleared my throat, but still my voice was hoarse and broken. "And I'd like to be one, but I can't fly all over the world killing people. I don't—"

"Oh God, no," Darius gasped, almost laughing. "I don't—I can't take jobs like that anymore. I'm the vault."

"Which means what?"

"To you it will mean that you'll go with me if I have to pick something up or drop something off, and that part will be mostly easy."

"Why's that?"

"Because right now, if anything happened to me, no one knows where their art or jewelry or paintings or precious stones or poison gas or money... so much money, you have no idea... no one would know where that is."

"So people give you things to hide and keep safe, and even they don't know where," Brin surmised. "Is that it? The vault isn't a place: it's you."

"It's me," he conceded.

"So it's in everyone's best interest to keep you alive and breathing."

"It is."

"So if Grigor Jankovic hurt you or killed you—"

"His entire family would be erased."

"Starting with him."

Darius gave a quick nod.

"May I ask why you killed Grigor's men, then?" Pravi inquired. "You could have simply told Grigor that you were the vault, and he would have called his men off."

"I put a note in the envelope when I took the judge's diary—journal, log, ledger, whatever you want to call it—so Grigor was aware of who he was tangling with when he decided to stay the course and try and kill you all," Darius said.

"He never got the package," I explained. "I did."

"You did?"

I nodded.

Darius thought for a moment. "When you opened the package, did you read the note?"

"I did."

"Did you read it to Grigor?"

"Yes."

"So he was made aware of the fact that I had the ledger."

"He was."

"Then you see, he should have stopped at that point. There was no reason for him to pursue the matter any further."

"He might not have believed me."

"All he had to do was check. It's easy. Anyone who knows about the vault can search the member site to see if a particular item or items has been acquired."

"You can just google that?"

His lip curled at the corner. "No, not exactly. You need special software—"

"Like Tor or something like that."

"Yes. And once you have that, you can access the dark web. Then you find the vault site, and from there you can search for the specific item you're looking for."

"You have to type it in, then, there's no master list."

"Correct. If the item has been acquired by the vault, then it's listed with the date that it was appropriated."

"And Grigor has access to all that."

"Yes."

"How do you know?"

"Because as the site manager, I know when people are tromping around in my house looking for something."

"Which he was."

"Which he was," Darius repeated.

"Then without a doubt he knew that you had the judge's ledger, but he came after me and Brin anyway."

"Yes."

"And so to make the point that you don't put up with that kinda shit, you made fifteen men simply vanish."

"I did."

"Leaving Grigor to explain what happened to them."

"Thanks to Marko, that won't be the only explaining Grigor needs to do today, but yes, that's precisely how things unfolded."

Pravi leaned back so he was shoulder to shoulder with me. "That doesn't inspire faith, Mr. Hawthorne. I'm not sure I can trust you."

"Oh, no, you can't," Darius insisted, agreeing with Pravi's assessment. "You trust Ceaton, and in turn, Ceaton trusts me because I trust him. After today I won't ever see you or talk to you, and if you ever do see me, you should run."

I heard Pravi suck in a breath.

"Because if you see me, that means either you did something to compromise Ceaton and he's dead and I'm coming for you, or it means that Ceaton turned on me and I'm eliminating his circle before I take him."

I knew neither scenario would ever occur, I wouldn't let it, but it was apparently not in Darius Hawthorne to beat around the bush or not explain every contingency. Everything was up front, cards on the table, and crystal clear so no one could get the wrong impression. And all of it, everything he said, calmed me because I believed him. I had faith in him, and standing on solid ground after having the rug pulled out from under me clicked everything back in place, like the world had righted itself.

"Is that clear?" he asked Pravi.

"Yes," he answered.

"It is good to know where one stands," Marko told him.

Darius turned to him. "I agree," he said, lacing his fingers together, resting his elbows on his thighs, still leaning forward, regarding us all. "Basically, I need Ceaton to work for me, and I'm not taking no for an answer."

I understood that already. I think we all did.

"He needs you all to have his back, and so I need you as well."

That too was evident.

"I've fixed this problem for him, and therefore you, Mr. Todd, as well as Mr. Radic, Mr. Borodin, and for Mr. Novak and Mr. Novak's mother."

Yes, he had. And including Luka's mother, who was like Team Mom since Pravi had lost his years ago as well, went a long way to solidifying trust.

"You're all safe because of me."

No arguing with his logic. He had us all good and caught. But for once, that didn't feel like a bad thing. This man knew me already, knew who I was, what I'd done, and had come in search of me because he was building a team and wanted me not only on it, but heading it up. I was both grateful and overwhelmed at the same time.

"I'm sorry I couldn't save your father, the judge," Darius admitted to Brin. "But you have to remember… he made his bed, and I understand you weren't close."

"We weren't, no."

"But this way you can know that because Ceaton works for me, your parents, the artists, your mother who works in glass and your father who paints, are utterly safe."

"You don't miss anything," I murmured. It was scary how much he knew. His knowledge coming off as almost arrogant. I'd once thought that Grigor was a powerful man, and now I realized what power truly looked like. It was impossible to not be impressed by the man, by both the coldness and absolutes that he worked with, the entire black and white of his existence. There was no good or bad with him, only those on the right side of him and those on the wrong.

What was slightly scary was that he passed judgment and saw nothing wrong with playing God.

"No," he agreed. "I don't."

I was startled momentarily, thinking he'd read my mind somehow. "I—"

"Normally," Darius said quickly, and I understood then what he was actually responding to. "I'm on top of everything. But you see, that's why I need you to look out for me and make certain that if I do make a mistake, I have a safety net in place to ensure the fall is a short one."

I nodded.

"I've been doing things myself for a very long time, and I've made this recent change so I can watch over a friend, as I said, and keep my reputation intact at the same time."

"Your reputation?"

"For being a dangerous man."

I had no doubt he was more than that; I suspected he was altogether grave.

"And Mr. Todd—"

"Brin," he corrected my new boss. "Please."

"Brin," Darius repeated. "I want you to know that I'll have your sweet little house all back in one piece by tomorrow morning with everything in it as good as new."

"Thank you."

"I'm sorry I can't say the same about your apartment," he said to me.

"What?" I said, my tone sharper than I meant.

"Grigor tossed your place and then torched it. I see a lot of clothes shopping in your future."

"Are you kidding?" I gasped. "All my stuff is gone?"

He winced, clearly sorry.

Still, it made some freakish sense with the rest of the day I was having. Of course I would have lost all my possessions. I had to start with a clean slate.

At least I had my watch and my coat and a duffel bag packed for three days.

"Jesus, he really did turn on me in a heartbeat."

"That's how it normally is," Darius said with a shrug. "But the good news is your guns were in your personal safe at the gun range you frequent, so they escaped the destruction."

"Yeah, that was lucky. I'll have to find a new place by—"

"Or you can just stay with Brin," Darius reasoned, then yawned quickly, leaning back on the couch. "As I said, his place will be in good shape by the morning."

"I—"

"That's a great idea," Brin agreed eagerly, all smiles, hand between my shoulder blades. "And that way you'll know exactly where to find him."

"Always," Darius agreed. He passed me the box he'd set on the couch beside him. It was covered with beautiful black lacquer and pearl inlay.

I looked at him, wondering what I was supposed to do.

"Open it," he said, like it should have been obvious.

Lifting the lid, I found three stacks of money and an Iridium satellite phone.

"The money is for you and your men," he informed me, his tone flat, delivering instructions like all military men did, sharply, succinctly, and without pause. "I'll have bank accounts set up by tomorrow, but you'll need to have funds wired to you from now on, as the accounts will be out of the country."

"Understood."

"The phone is programmed with my number in it so you can always reach me, and I need you to keep it on you at all times."

"Roger that," I replied fast, the words out of my mouth before I even thought about them. These were orders I was receiving, and so I responded as I'd been trained to do.

His grin was quick, curling his lip, softening his eyes. "You need a bag ready to grab and go. Once you replace your wardrobe, make sure you have one packed."

"Yessir, I will."

"You—"

"This box is beautiful," Brin interrupted, cooing over the thing, smoothing his hand across the open lid. "It's from the Joseon Dynasty, right?"

"It is. You have a good eye."

Brin beamed over at my new boss. "I have a covered bowl from the Goryeo Dynasty at home that I really hope didn't get hit by any stray bullets."

"That would be a tragedy," Darius said soberly, his brows pinched as he regarded Brin.

Men were dead, but a piece of pottery being destroyed—that would be *bad*? These were priorities I didn't understand. Perhaps that was why me being at the top, making life-and-death decisions, was not where my strength lay. I needed to make sure Darius and everyone else on my team, and Brin, stayed safe. That was a mission I could get behind.

"I really hope it made it," Brin sighed, "but everything I really wanted safe is right here with me, and that's all because of you."

He met Darius's stare and held it.

"Thank you."

"You're quite welcome." Darius rose then, and Brin did too, scrambling out of his seat to rush over and offer his hand.

They shook quickly, and then I passed Brin the box that was apparently a much bigger deal than I understood. To me it was pretty; I had no idea it was art. Apparently I had a lot to learn about a great many things.

I swallowed hard and faced Darius. "Thank you for saving all of our lives, and for looking for me, and for giving me a chance. I promise I won't let you down."

"I have no doubt," Darius made known, clapping me on the shoulder before he departed, closing the front door on his way out.

Pravi stood up beside me and held out his hand, waiting.

Brin passed me a wad of money that I gave to him. His sly grin made me smile in spite of how serious I was trying to be.

"You're still not the boss."

"Yeah, I know."

He tapped my chest with the bills. "You are my brother."

I knew that too.

"And I will work with you and watch your back as well."

"Thank you."

"*Nema na čemu*," he answered and then held his hand out again.

"What?"

"For Luka," he said simply.

"You'll make sure he's safe? You'll go talk to him?"

"He's already safe," Pravi assured me. "You know that. But yes, I'll go to the hospital now and explain things to him."

"Thank you."

He nodded and stepped up to me, wrapped an arm around my neck, and hugged me tight for just a moment. When he pulled back, he kissed my cheek and then stepped aside, waiting as Marko took his place in front of me.

Brin gave me a wad for him too.

"I will go with Pravi to check on Luka, as well as his mother. We will come by your home tomorrow," Marko apprised me, giving me a quick smack on the chest before he walked with Pravi to the front door.

"No, you just heard Darius. My apartment was torched."

"At your home with Brinley, you idiot," Pravi said as he reached the door, opened it, and left without another word.

"Try and follow what is happening," Marko cautioned me, shaking his head as he closed the door behind him.

"He's giving me shit," I told Brin. "Motherfucker."

"Everyone in your life is so cool," Brin exclaimed as he walked around in front of me. "They all leave a room so well."

I looked at him, staring at his beautiful little pixie face, the puffy pink lips, perfectly arched brows, and those daring dimples. He was so sweet and so patient and so kind. It was difficult to grasp that at this exact moment, we were perfectly and completely safe. Running through everything that had happened in this one short day, letting all the events tumble around in my head, made it hard to look away from him. We'd been on a journey together, been partners, and I couldn't imagine ever being parted from him.

The thought was scary and important and so very heavy, weighted as it was with decisions for the future and unspoken plans.

I was drowning right there in front of him, at a total loss for words.

He waggled his eyebrows at me, and the water receded and I came up for air.

"You're insane. Why aren't you running away as fast as you can?"

Brin gestured at the door. "Well, I can't now. I think that Mr. Hawthorne thought I was really important to you since he just explained about the vault and how he kills people really easy, and how he needs you to make sure no one sneaks up behind him and offs him while he's offing someone else."

"Oh yeah?" I asked, threading my fingers through his thick, curling, wavy mane that I found myself enjoying the feel of the more I touched it. The pink apples of his cheeks, long and thick lashes, and his cute little button nose were all a wonder to me. The way his eyes sparkled with mischief and heat, how he leaned into me, bumped me with his hip, touched me with those beautiful hands, bit his bottom lip as he was gazing up at me like he was drunk and sighing as though I was doing something amazing just standing there—it was all just…. God… it was *home*, and I wanted to step in and just *be* there. I wanted to claim what he was offering and have it be done.

"Yeah," he whispered, lifting up on his toes and wrapping his arms around my neck and easing me down, as he tilted his chin up. "He'll kill me if you don't come live with me. He thinks we're together already, and he's really, really scary."

"I'm scary," I suggested, kissing his forehead, the tip of his nose, and his cheek.

"You're not," he assured me before he let out a long, low whimper. "You're just mine."

I took him then.

I kissed him breathless, held him tight, bowed his back, and pressed him to me so he could feel my cock, the hardness and heft, grinding into his thigh.

"You're safe, I'm safe," he whispered as I lifted him off his feet and up into my arms, my hands on his ass, his legs wrapped around my hips as I carried him through the house, looking for and finding the bedroom where Brin had dumped his overnight bag when we arrived. "You have nowhere to go, nowhere to be, nothing to do except me."

"Oh, that was terrible," I moaned, loving that after everything that had occurred today, he could still resort to truly horrible puns.

He murmured something as he kissed my throat, wriggling in my arms, trying to get closer before he kissed me, and there was nothing, only heat and need and me taking and him yielding. I wasn't going to hold back a moment longer; it was useless when, clearly, I belonged to him.

He knew I was his, recognized it even before I did, and arguing with a man who so knew his own mind was madness.

I tried to be gentle with his clothes; he tore at mine. When I put my gun on the nightstand, I realized the weapon turned him on big-time from the way he stared.

"Got a gun kink, do you?" I teased him.

"It's because it's yours," he rasped, panting beneath me, and it hit me that everything about me pushed all his buttons and that, in and of itself, was a wonder.

The wings of the raven stretched across his chest and back, looking as though it were ready to take flight, stunning in the black and gray ink. And there was in flowing script down his side, over his ribs: *Aut viam inveniam au faciam.*

"What does that mean?" I asked as I kissed my way over the words, licking, biting.

He bowed up off the bed, shivering with fresh need. "I shall either find a way or make one."

"That's deep," I said against his skin, nibbling over his navel for a moment before traveling lower.

"Ceaton!"

I yanked down his pants and briefs—the belt, button, and zipper surrendering to my deft fingers—and swallowed his long, pretty cock down the back of my throat.

"Fuck!" he roared, and it was a good sound, one of absolute blinding joy and complete and utter submission. As I sucked and licked, made everything wet and let him fuck my mouth, I slid saliva-slicked fingers into his ass, opening him up, unrelenting in my attention. As he came apart in my hands, he started speaking in Latin.

I loved it. A lot.

"I've never," he gasped, "no one ever—I didn't—ohmygod!"

I was his first blow job?

There was no way not to ask. Letting him slip free, I looked up into those eyes of his now with blown pupils and glistening with tears. "The fuck are you talking about, your first blow job?"

"Nobody ever—guys said it was gross and they didn't want to taste the... the—"

"Cum?" I offered. "No one wanted to drink down your jizz?"

He shook his head.

"I do," I promised, laving him from balls to head. "I want it all."

"Fuck!" he shouted, and I laughed before I swallowed him again, messy and strong, loving the taste and feel and smell of him, using my hand, squeezing, tugging until he grabbed hold of my head and used me, lost completely until the scream tore from his chest and he spilled, hot and thick, down the back of my throat.

I had to crawl up over him and grab him tight, crush him to my chest as he shuddered in the safety of my arms. It took long moments for him to recover, and I kissed him the whole time, mauling his mouth, holding him still, sharing his taste with him until he was writhing beneath me, clawing at my back, demanding more.

"Oh, Ceaton, please," he mewled. "Please, please, please don't stop yet. I want to know what it's like to be loved by you."

No one had ever wanted me like this man did; I'd never been needed so fiercely, had every part of me, body and soul, laid claim to. I would give him anything he ever asked of me.

"Baby—"

He took a deep, shaky breath as he clutched at my shoulders, digging his fingers into the muscles of my back. "I want you buried in me, Ceaton. I want that now."

"Honey, I don't even know if there's lube here to—"

"I brought it; I put it in the nightstand."

True to his word, when I checked the drawer, it was there, but no condoms. "We're missing something."

"I'm good. I've never gone without a rubber. Have you?"

"You cannot take my word for that," I insisted.

"I can, I will. I know you're a good man, so tell me, is it safe?"

Of course it was. I never let anyone near me without one. "Yes," I said honestly, deeply humbled by his faith, by what he was offering me, and the leap he was taking. "I swear."

He exhaled fast. "Thank God, now have me, make me yours."

"We need to slow down. I don't want to hurt—"

"If you don't get inside me now, I will throw you on the ground and take what I want."

It was an interesting threat, considering I had easily a hundred pounds of muscle on him, but his point was well made. He had to have me, and that knowledge, how adamant he was, how possessive, the claim he was making, all of it, was a completely new experience, and I wanted to savor every moment of it. I couldn't get enough of this man who was not passive in the least, instead telling me what he wanted, demanding my surrender.

"Brin—"

"Don't you dare say no to me," he rasped, almost angry, utterly intent. "Listen to me instead, don't try to think for me or put yourself in my place, and if I say I want something—you need to give it to me."

I had to have the same faith in him he had in me.

Opening the lube, I slathered my hard, dripping cock and then tossed the bottle away as I took hold of his legs, lifted them to my shoulders, curled over him, and then pressed inside of him slowly but without stopping, feeling that tight ring of muscle expand around me. I watched his face, checking, being careful, but still driving, filling him, stretching him, sliding my palms over his skin, the ridge of his hipbone catching on the webbing of my thumb as I kept my gaze locked with his the whole time I entered him.

If being in bed with the wrong person could shatter you, could being with the right one change your life?

"Oh yes," he moaned decadently, bucking under me, trying to take me in deeper, arching his back as I took hold of his cock and stroked languorously.

Just looking at him—ravaged, sweat glistening on his hot, gilded skin, flushed with passion, trembling as I pushed inside of him—stole my reason. I shoved in deeper with each new thrust until I lost my rhythm, needing to come, having to use him, the choice stripped from me as my brain shut down and a wild, raw, wanton craving took hold.

He chanted my name, the begging endless, and I pounded him through his second climax of the night and my first.

I collapsed on top of him, pinning him under me, and I lay there in a sticky, sated sprawl, not caring at the moment that he probably couldn't breathe. The laughter was a surprise.

When I eased from his body and rolled over on my back, he scrambled up against my side, laid his head over my heart, and I tucked him closer, tighter, kissing his sweaty head and then his lips when he lifted for my mouth.

"Ohmygod, if you lie and say that wasn't the best sex you ever had, I—"

"That was the best sex I ever had," I said, chuckling, then kissed him again, unable to stop hugging him, wanting him melded to me, in me, wanting us to be one thing, one heart... just *one*.

"You're going to love living with me," he said between kisses, squirming in my arms, twisting, looking for a position he liked.

I lifted up, shoving him under me again, and then came down on top of him as he parted his thighs and I rested between them. I couldn't help thinking it was where I belonged.

"And tomorrow I'm going to take off from school and go clothes shopping with you. It'll be fun, and then we'll come home and fool around and sleep and watch movies and then fool around again, and—"

"We gotta do more than fuck," I told him. "We have to talk and plan, because it's important that we're on the same page."

"Oh, I agree," he granted, sounding suspiciously placating even as he shifted beneath me, and my cock, already hardening, slid against his slick entrance. "We'll do so much more talking, I swear."

He was a greedy thing and I loved it. We fit perfectly, and that made all the sense in the world after how life-altering the day had been.

What a difference a day makes—I'd always heard that and never believed it. But now I knew better. Now I would never take time for granted, any, at all, ever again. It was too precious, as was the man in bed with me. He was a gift, and I would make the most of every second.

"Ceaton... baby... can you hold me tighter?"

I could and would for as long as he'd let me.

MARY CALMES lives in Lexington, Kentucky, with her husband and two children and loves all the seasons except summer. She graduated from the University of the Pacific in Stockton, California, with a bachelor's degree in English literature. Due to the fact that it is English lit and not English grammar, do not ask her to point out a clause for you, as it will so not happen. She loves writing, becoming immersed in the process, and believes without question in happily-ever-afters, and writes those for each and every one of her characters.

OLD LOYALTY, NEW LOVE

MARY CALMES

L'Ange: Book One

When jackal shifter Quade Danas was banished from his pack for being gay, he spent years in the military escaping his father's prejudice before returning to civilian life as a bodyguard for Roman Howell, the teenage son of a very rich man. After Roman is in an accident that leaves him physically scarred and emotionally distant, Quade is the only one who can get through to him. As Roman becomes a man, he realizes what he wants—his bodyguard by his side and in his bed. Unfortunately, Quade can't seem to see past the kid Roman once was to the man he has become, certain Roman's feelings are merely misplaced gratitude. But Roman knows a lot more than Quade realizes, and he's used to persevering, no matter how many impediments life throws his way. He wants the chance to prove to Quade that he's strong enough for a jackal alpha to call mate.

Despite the decades Quade has been away, and the heartache of his father's rejection, his inborn loyalty to the pack remains, and his abrupt departure left the jackal shifters without an alpha heir. As a psychopath shifter staking claim as alpha draws Quade back home, and Quade feels compelled to heed the call, he may be forced to make a choice he never anticipated. But doing so means he must leave Roman behind… unless somehow they find a way to make loyalty and love work together.

www.dreamspinnerpress.com

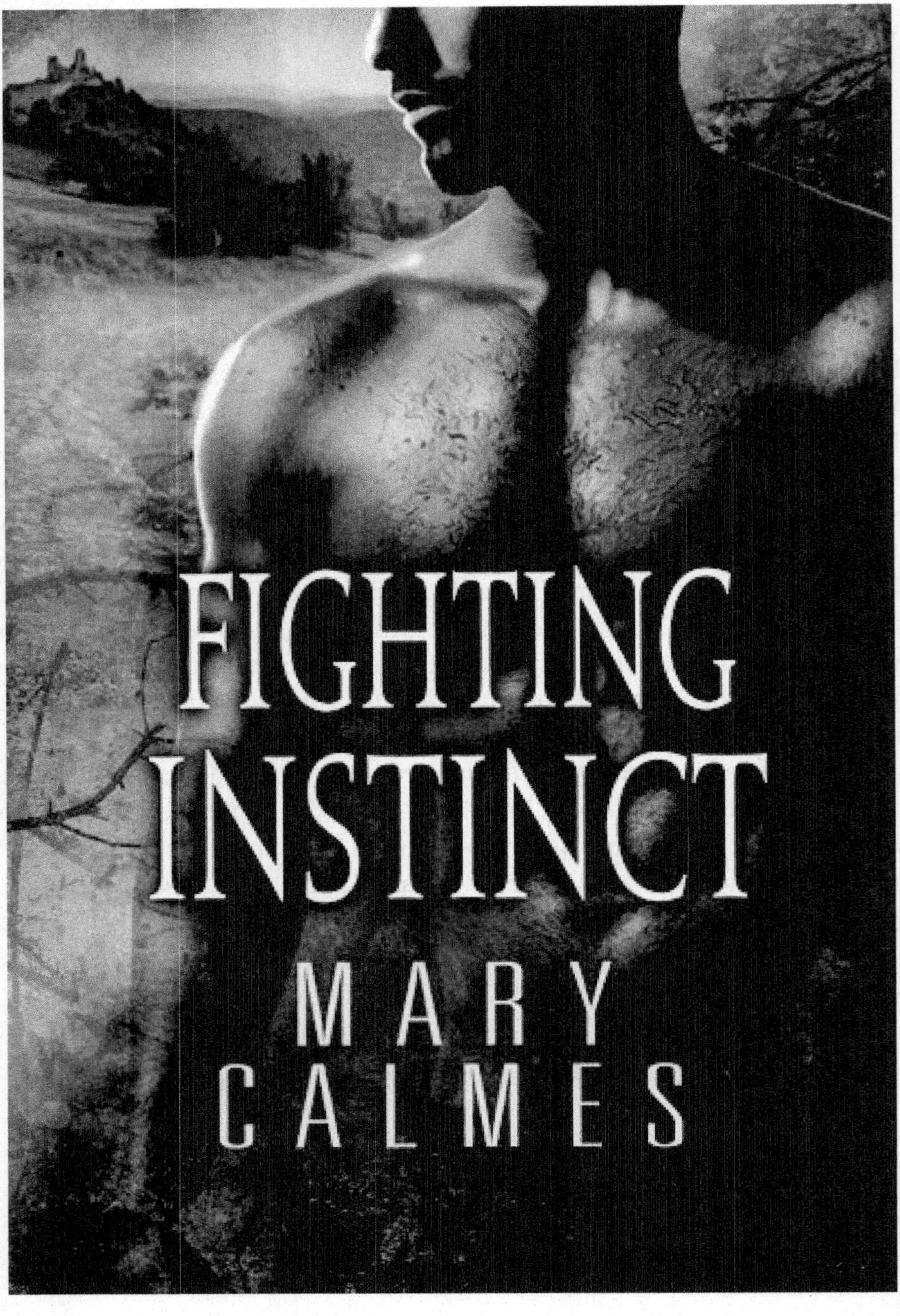
FIGHTING
INSTINCT
MARY
CALMES

L'Ange: Book Two

Only a privileged few know L'Ange's head of security Arman de Soto is a shifter, and even fewer know he's been systematically killing off a pack of werewolves. The reason for this vengeance is a secret Arman trusts with no one, quite the opposite of his obvious longtime pursuit of the château's overseer, Linus Hobbes. Despite Arman's reputation as a loner, the only thing he needs to complete his life is Linus. Predator and prey just don't mix—but Arman won't give him up.

Linus has lived alone for more than seven years, sheltered at L'Ange under an assumed name and hiding secrets of his own, including his terrifying attraction to the most dangerous man he's ever met. Arman knows Linus should be afraid of the predator stalking him, but Linus is still drawn to him like a moth to a flame, no matter how much he tries to deny his instincts. It's not until Linus's past and Arman's crusade exposes their secrets and opens L'Ange to attack that Arman realizes waiting any longer is a risk he just can't take. So he'll have to take his quest to the source of the threat in a gamble to protect L'Ange, Linus, and any future they might have together.

www.dreamspinnerpress.com

CHOSEN
PRIDE

MARY
CALMES

L'Ange: Book Three

Jon Slade finally met his mate, but instead of it being the happiest day of his life, it became the saddest when wolf shifter Kelvin MacCurdy chose his obligations over their fated bond, leaving Jon to pick up the pieces of his shattered dreams. Lucky for him, Roman Howell, his boss and the owner of L'Ange, saw promise in the forlorn lion and put him to work so he wouldn't have time to sit around and lick his wounds while he waited for his wounded spirit to heal.

Then the wolves make an official visit to L'Ange, and Jon finds out Kelvin's pining for him is taking its toll on his position as the king's champion. Though Kelvin's training and the expectations of others steer him toward an intended mate, Jon has an unbreakable hold on his heart, and it's no longer possible for Kelvin to keep himself from where he truly belongs.

But the conclave brings more than Kelvin to the château. It also brings a challenge to jackal alpha Quade Danas, a threat that Quade and Roman, Arman and Linus, and Jon and Kelvin may have to fight in order to keep L'Ange's family intact. Jon never wanted to lead a pride, but the loyalty and devotion to one is ingrained in him. Kelvin was raised to punish anyone who questioned his king, but the calling to protect others runs through his veins just as deeply. To come out on the other side of the battle together, Jon and Kelvin will have to hold the darkness of solitary pride and broken hearts at bay—and find strength in belonging to something bigger than themselves.

www.dreamspinnerpress.com

TIMING

Mary Calmes

Timing: Book One

Stefan Joss just can't win. Not only does he have to go to Texas in the middle of summer to be the man of honor in his best friend Charlotte's wedding, but he's expected to negotiate a million-dollar business deal at the same time. Worst of all, he's thrown for a loop when he arrives to see the one man Charlotte promised wouldn't be there: her brother, Rand Holloway.

Stefan and Rand have been mortal enemies since the day they met, so Stefan is shocked when a temporary cease-fire sees the usual hostility replaced by instant chemistry. Though leery of the unexpected feelings, Stefan is swayed by a sincere revelation from Rand, and he decides to give Rand a chance.

But their budding romance is threatened when Stefan's business deal goes wrong: the owner of the last ranch he needs to secure for the company is murdered. Stefan's in for the surprise of his life as he finds himself in danger as well.

www.dreamspinnerpress.com

AFTER THE SUNSET

Mary Calmes

Timing: Book Two

Two years after riding off into the sunset with ranch owner Rand Holloway, Stefan Joss has made a tentative peace with his new life, teaching at a community college. But the course of true love never does run smooth. Rand wants him home on the ranch; Stef wants an exit strategy in case Rand ever decides to throw him out. Finally, after recognizing how unfair he's being, Stef makes a commitment, and Rand is over the moon.

When Stef gets the chance to prove his devotion, he doesn't hesitate—despite the risk to his health—and Rand takes the opportunity to show everyone that sometimes life's best surprises come after the sunset.

www.dreamspinnerpress.com

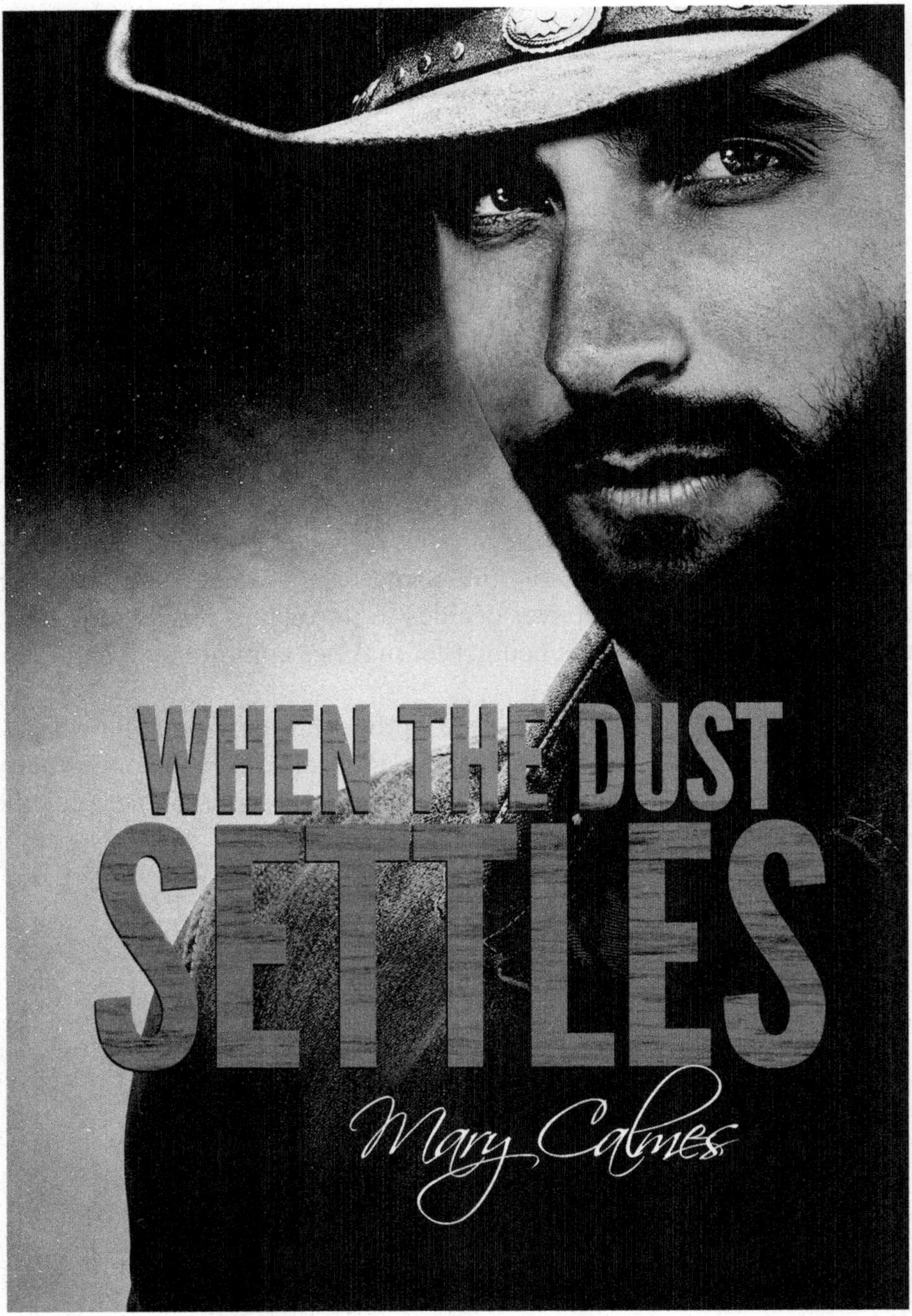
WHEN THE DUST
SETTLES
Mary Calmes

A Timing Story

Glenn Holloway's predictable life ended the day he confessed his homosexuality to his family. As if that wasn't enough, he then poured salt in the wound by walking away from the ranch he'd grown up on, to open the restaurant he'd always dreamed of. Without support from his father and brother, and too proud to accept assistance from anyone else, he had to start from scratch. Over time things worked out: Glenn successfully built a strong business, created a new home, and forged a life he could be proud of.

Despite his success, his estrangement from the Holloways is still a sore spot he can't quite heal, and a called-in favor becomes Glenn's worst nightmare. Caught in a promise, Glenn returns to his roots to deal with Rand Holloway and comes face-to-face with Mac Gentry, a man far too appealing for Glenn's own good. It could all lead to disaster— disaster for his tenuous reconnection with his family and for the desire he didn't know he held in his heart.

www.dreamspinnerpress.com

CPSIA information can be obtained
at www.ICGtesting.com
Printed in the USA
LVOW13s0325130417
530671LV00004B/51/P